LIMITED EDITION ALTERNATE COVER!

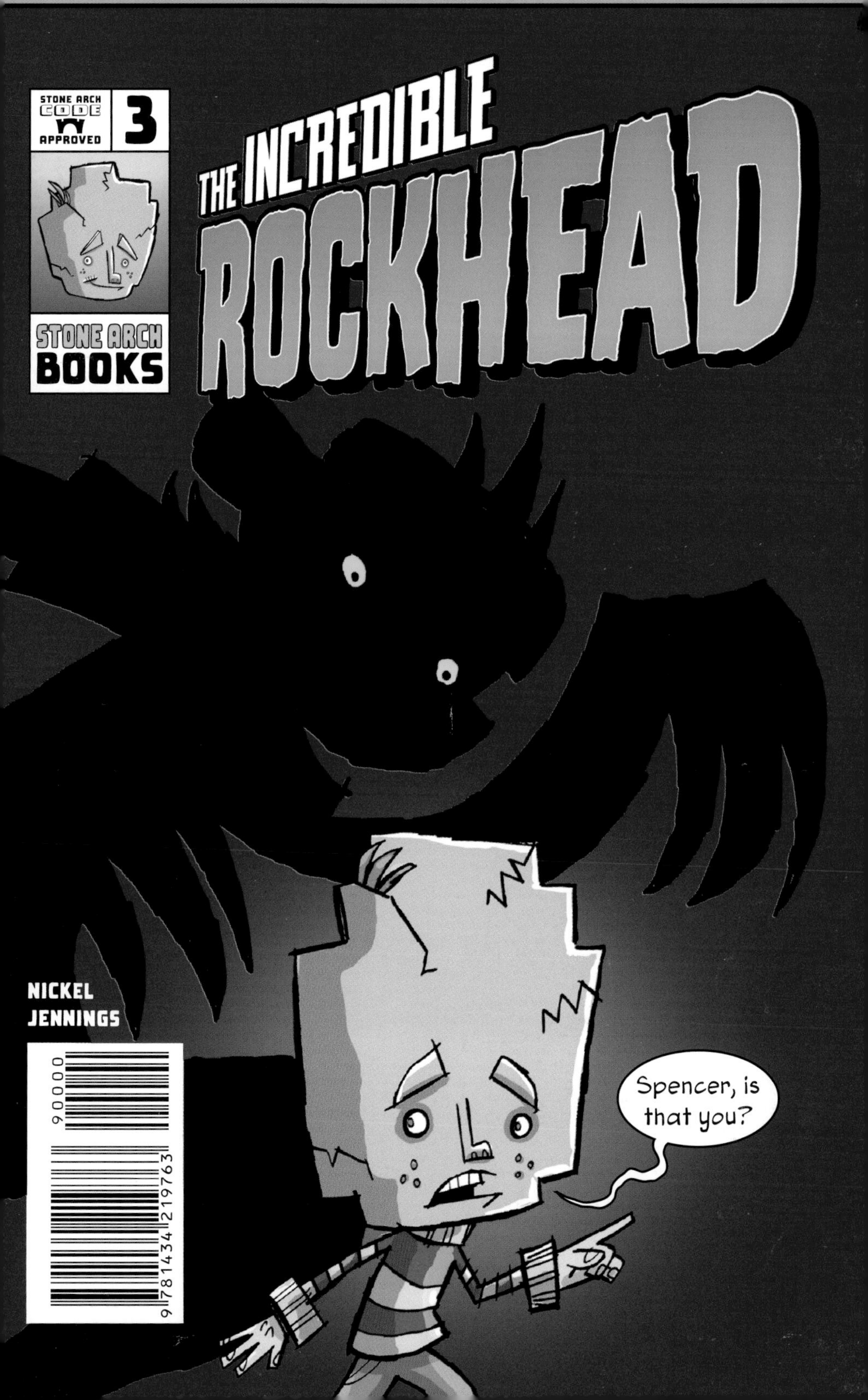
STONE ARCH CODE APPROVED
3
THE INCREDIBLE ROCKHEAD
STONE ARCH BOOKS
NICKEL
JENNINGS
Spencer, is that you?

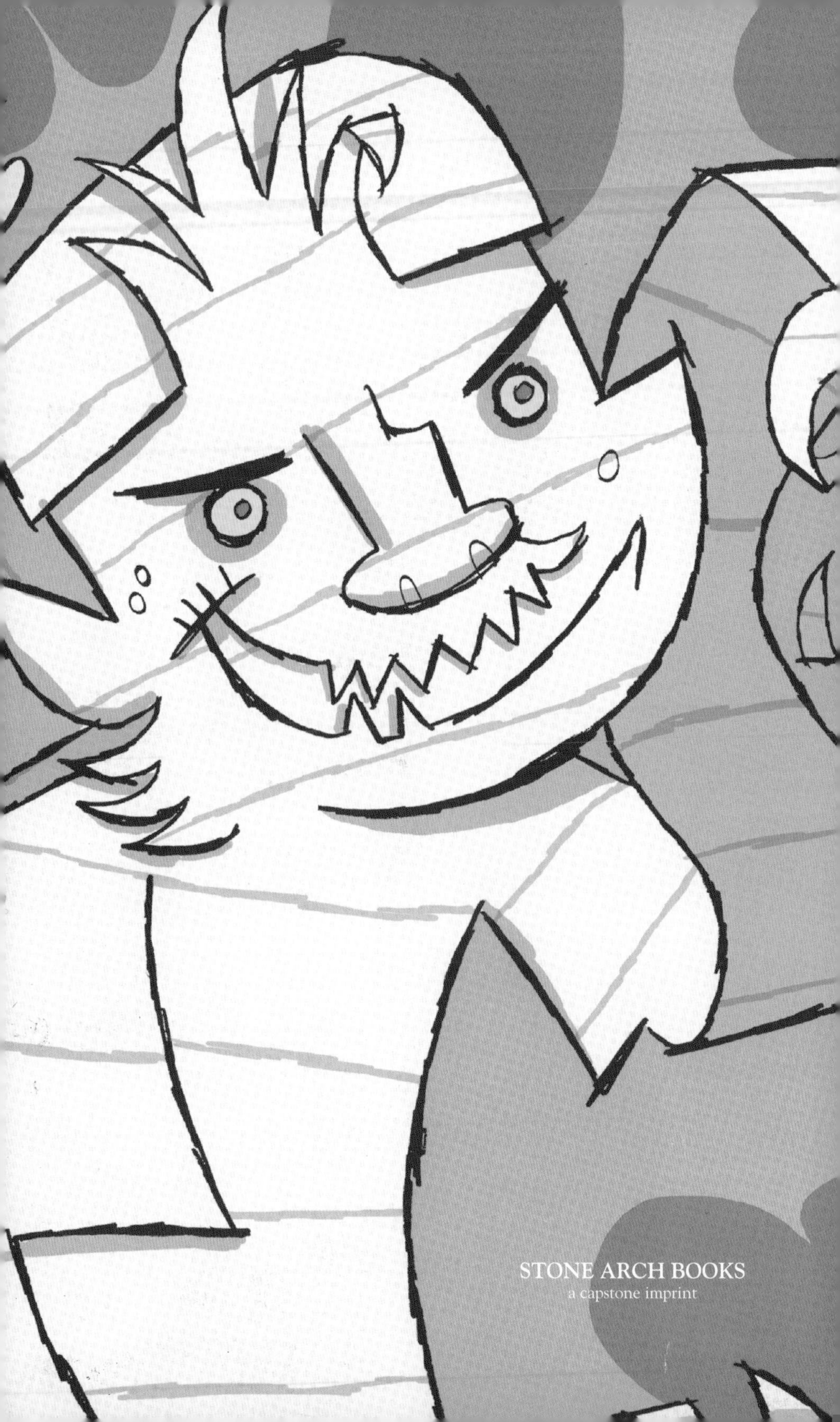

STONE ARCH BOOKS
a capstone imprint

THE INCREDIBLE ROCKHEAD VS. PAPERCUT!

WRITTEN BY **SCOTT NICKEL**

ILLUSTRATED BY **C.S. JENNINGS**

DESIGNER: **BOB LENTZ**

CREATIVE DIRECTOR: **HEATHER KINDSETH**

PRODUCTION SPECIALIST: **MICHELLE BIEDSCHEID**

SENIOR EDITOR: **DONALD LEMKE**

ASSOC. EDITOR: **SEAN TULIEN**

EDITORIAL DIRECTOR: **MICHAEL DAHL**

CASTING ASSOCIATE: STONE E. IYERS

HAIR STYLIST DEPARTMENT HEAD: ROXANNA HARDPLACE

WARDROBE SUPERVISOR: EDDIE BOULDER

STUNTS CHOREOGRAPHER: ROCKY CLIFFTON

STUNTPERSON 1: TEDDY AZIROK

KEY RIGGING GRIP: MICAH ROLLENSTONE

Graphic Sparks are published by Stone Arch Books, a Capstone Imprint, 151 Good Counsel Drive, P.O. Box 669 Mankato, Minnesota 56002
www.capstonepub.com Copyright © 2011 by Stone Arch Books All rights reserved. No part of this publication may be reproduced in whole
or in part, or stored in a retrieval system, or transmitted in any form or by any means, electronic, mechanical, photocopying, recording, or
otherwise, without written permission of the publisher.

Cataloging-in-Publication Data is available on the Library of Congress website.

ISBN: 978-1-4342-1976-3 (library binding)

Summary: Chip Stone, a.k.a. the Incredible Rockhead, has yet to meet his match — until now. Rockhead is up against an enemy designed to defeat
him — Papercut! With the entire school watching, this paper tiger is looking to cover Rockhead in the most action-packed game of paper, rock,
scissors the world has ever seen. Is this the end of our boulder-headed hero, or will Rock find a way to hammer Paper into pulp?

Printed in the United States of Ame
032010   005741WZF10

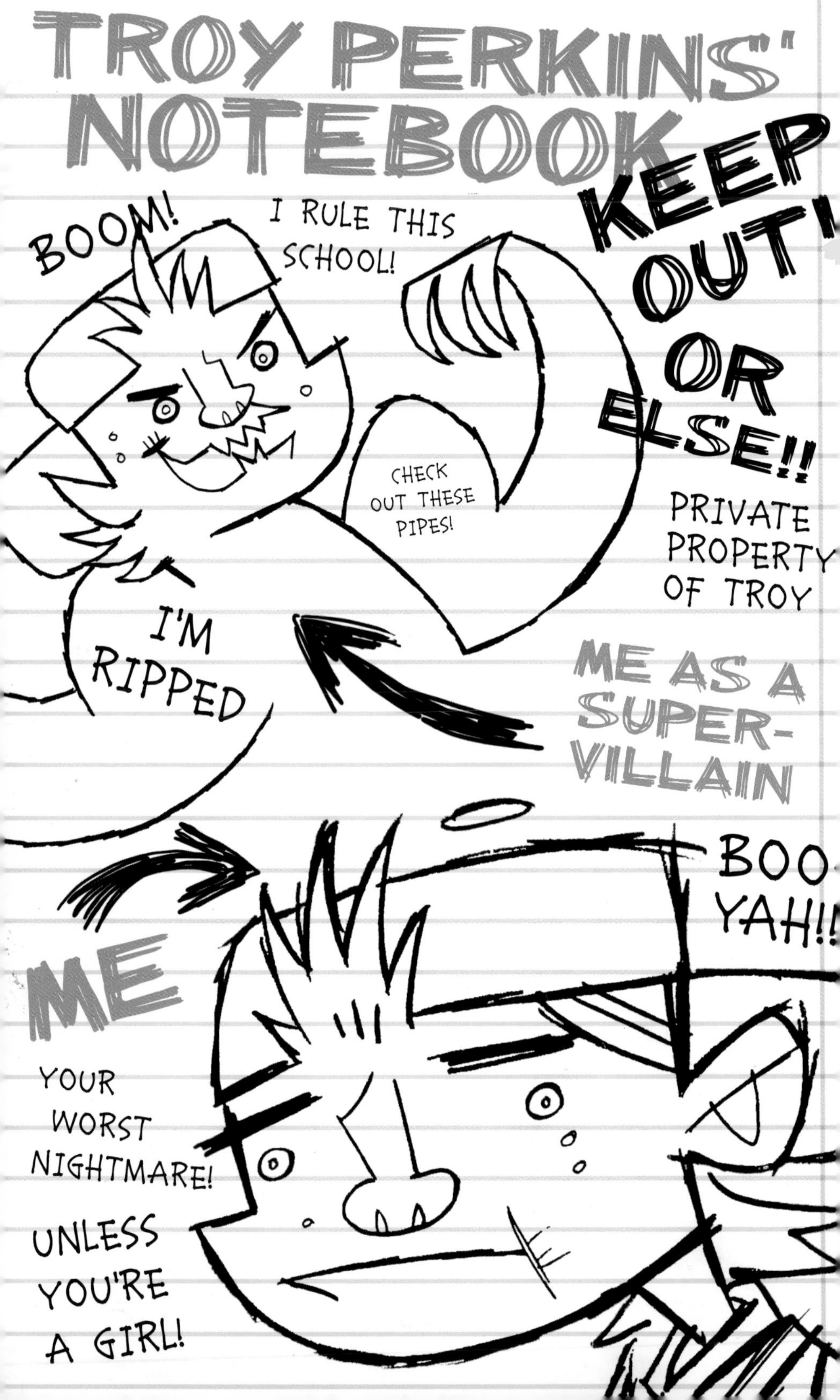
TROY PERKINS' NOTEBOOK
KEEP OUT! OR ELSE!!
BOOM!
I RULE THIS SCHOOL!
CHECK OUT THESE PIPES!
PRIVATE PROPERTY OF TROY
I'M RIPPED
ME AS A SUPER-VILLAIN
BOO YAH!!
ME
YOUR WORST NIGHTMARE!
UNLESS YOU'RE A GIRL!

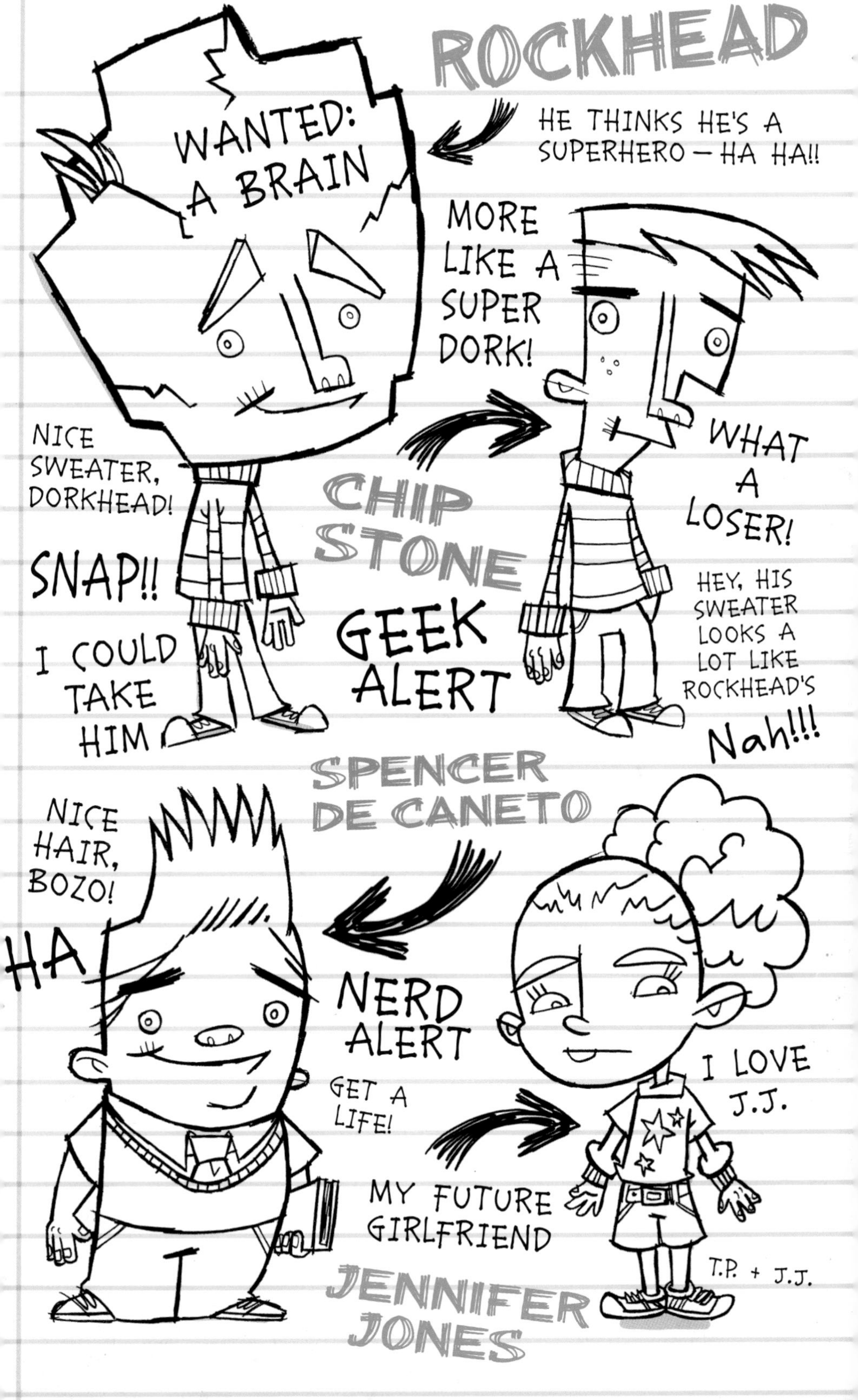
ROCKHEAD
HE THINKS HE'S A SUPERHERO — HA HA!!
WANTED: A BRAIN
MORE LIKE A SUPER DORK!
NICE SWEATER, DORKHEAD!
CHIP STONE
WHAT A LOSER!
SNAP!!
GEEK ALERT
HEY, HIS SWEATER LOOKS A LOT LIKE ROCKHEAD'S
I COULD TAKE HIM
Nah!!!
SPENCER DE CANETO
NICE HAIR, BOZO!
HA
NERD ALERT
GET A LIFE!
I LOVE J.J.
MY FUTURE GIRLFRIEND
T.P. + J.J.
JENNIFER JONES

STONE ARCH BOOKS PROUDLY PRESENTS:

THE INCREDIBLE ROCKHEAD VS. PAPERCUT!

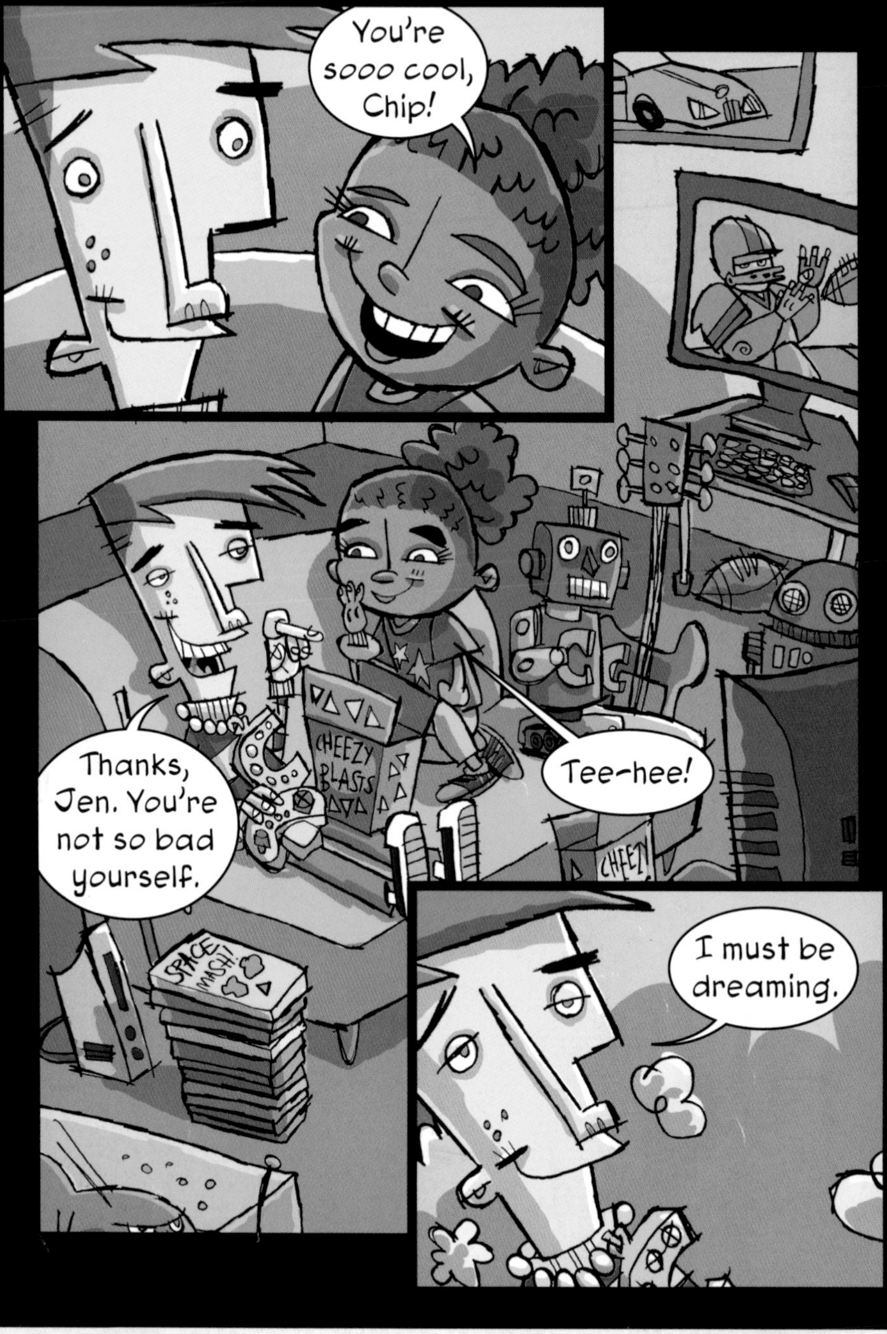
You're sooo cool, Chip!
Thanks, Jen. You're not so bad yourself.
Tee-hee!
CHEEZY BLASTS
SPACE MASH!
I must be dreaming.

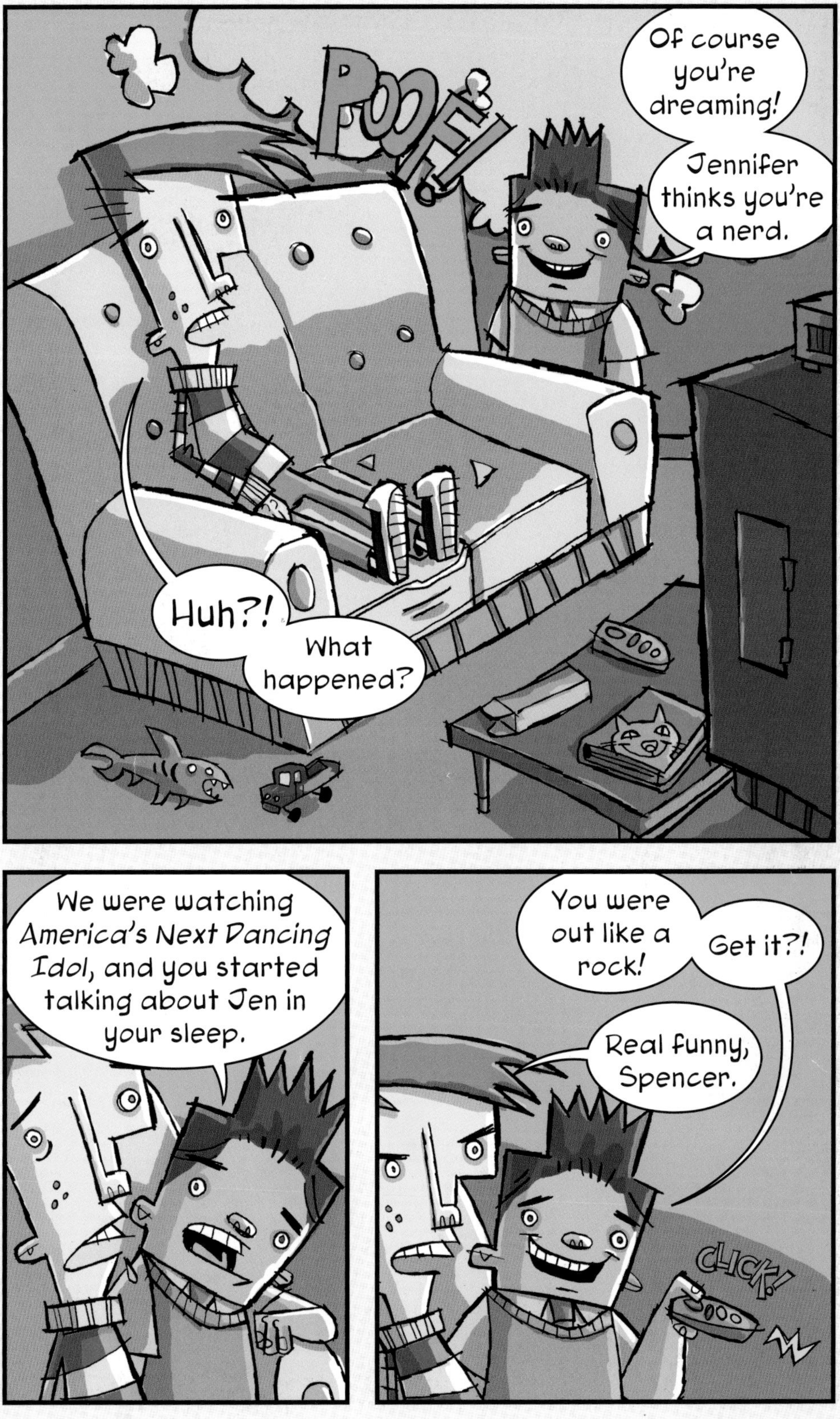
POOF!
Of course you're dreaming!
Jennifer thinks you're a nerd.
Huh?!
What happened?
We were watching *America's Next Dancing Idol*, and you started talking about Jen in your sleep.
You were out like a rock!
Get it?!
Real funny, Spencer.
CLICK!

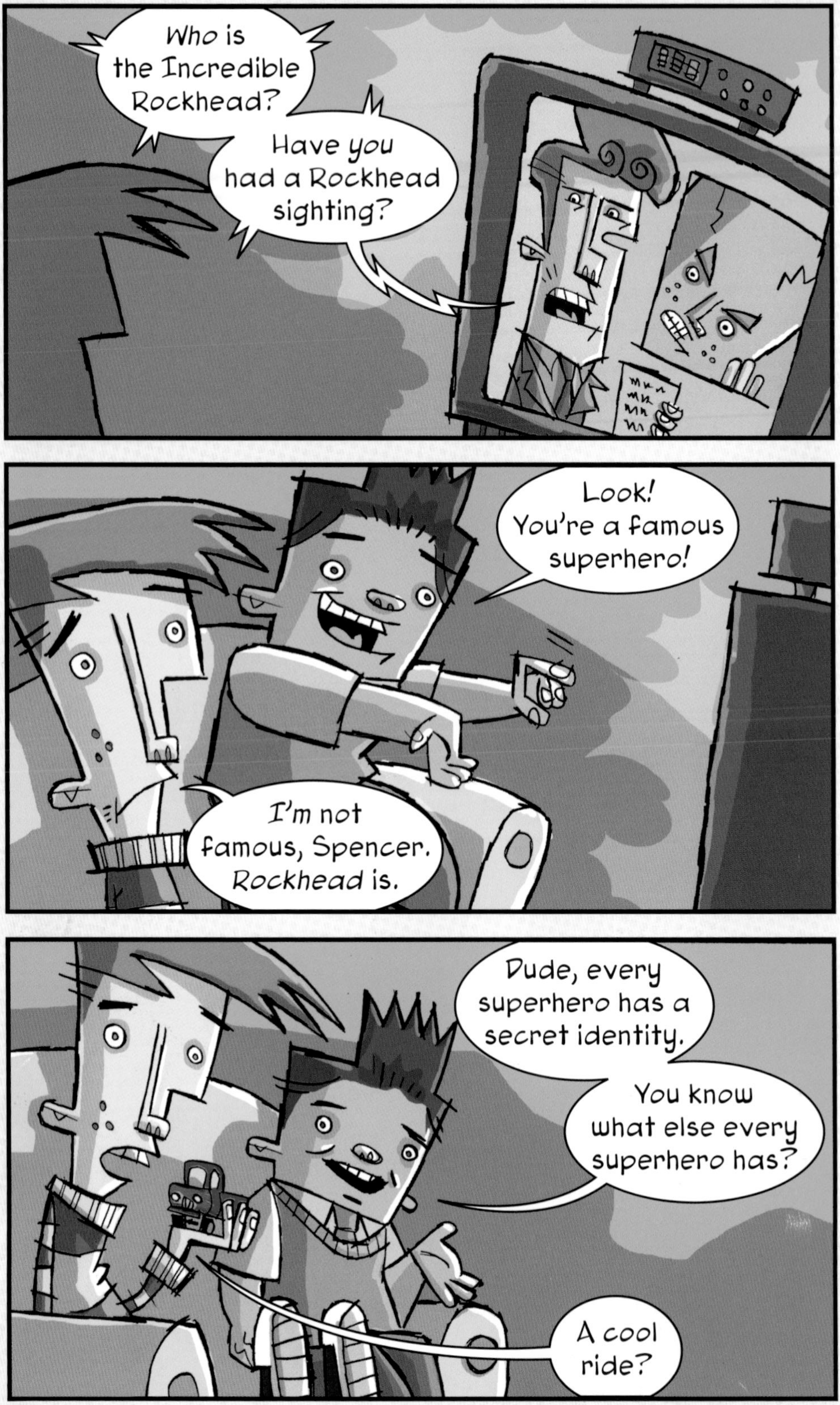
Who is the Incredible Rockhead?
Have you had a Rockhead sighting?
Look! You're a famous superhero!
I'm not famous, Spencer. Rockhead is.
Dude, every superhero has a secret identity.
You know what else every superhero has?
A cool ride?

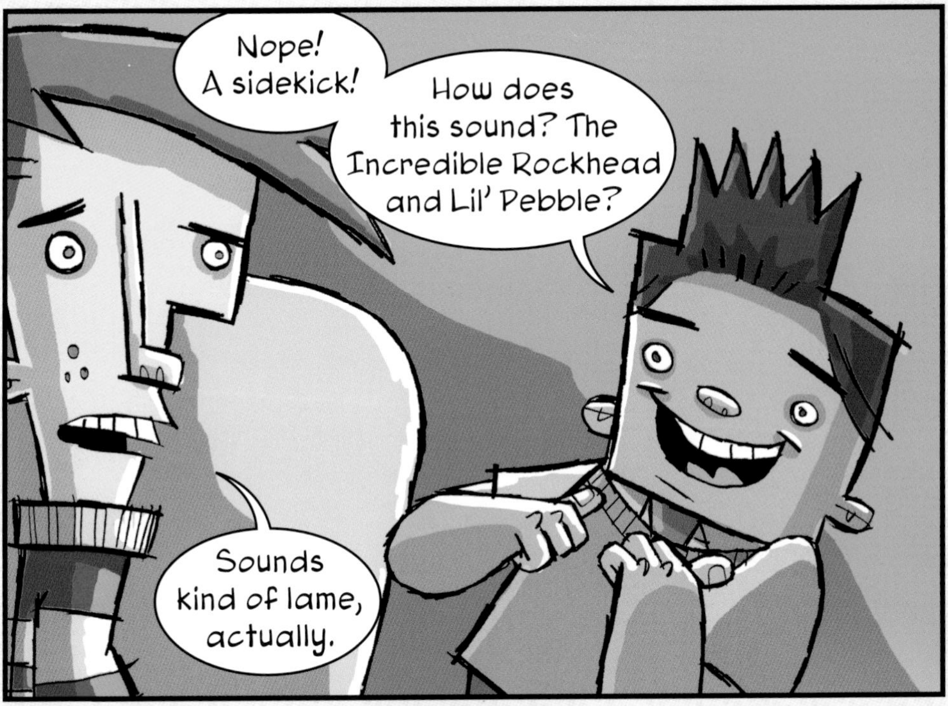
Nope!
A sidekick!
How does this sound? The Incredible Rockhead and Lil' Pebble?
Sounds kind of lame, actually.

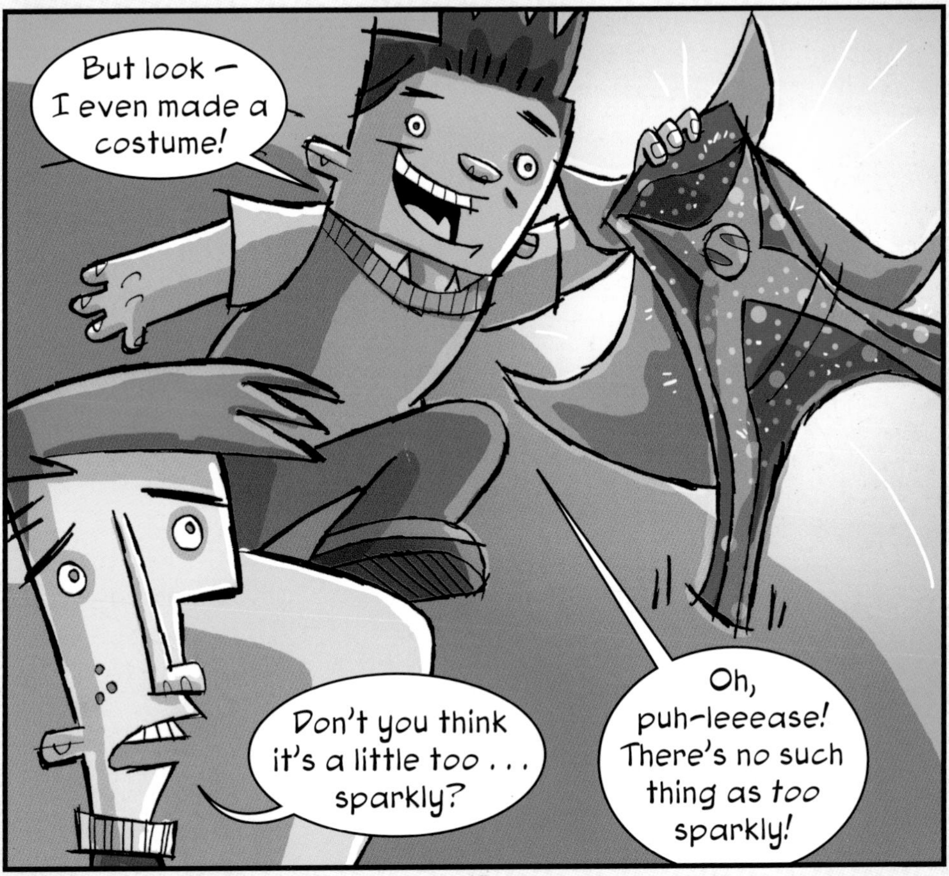
But look — I even made a costume!
Don't you think it's a little too . . . sparkly?
Oh, puh-leeease! There's no such thing as too sparkly!

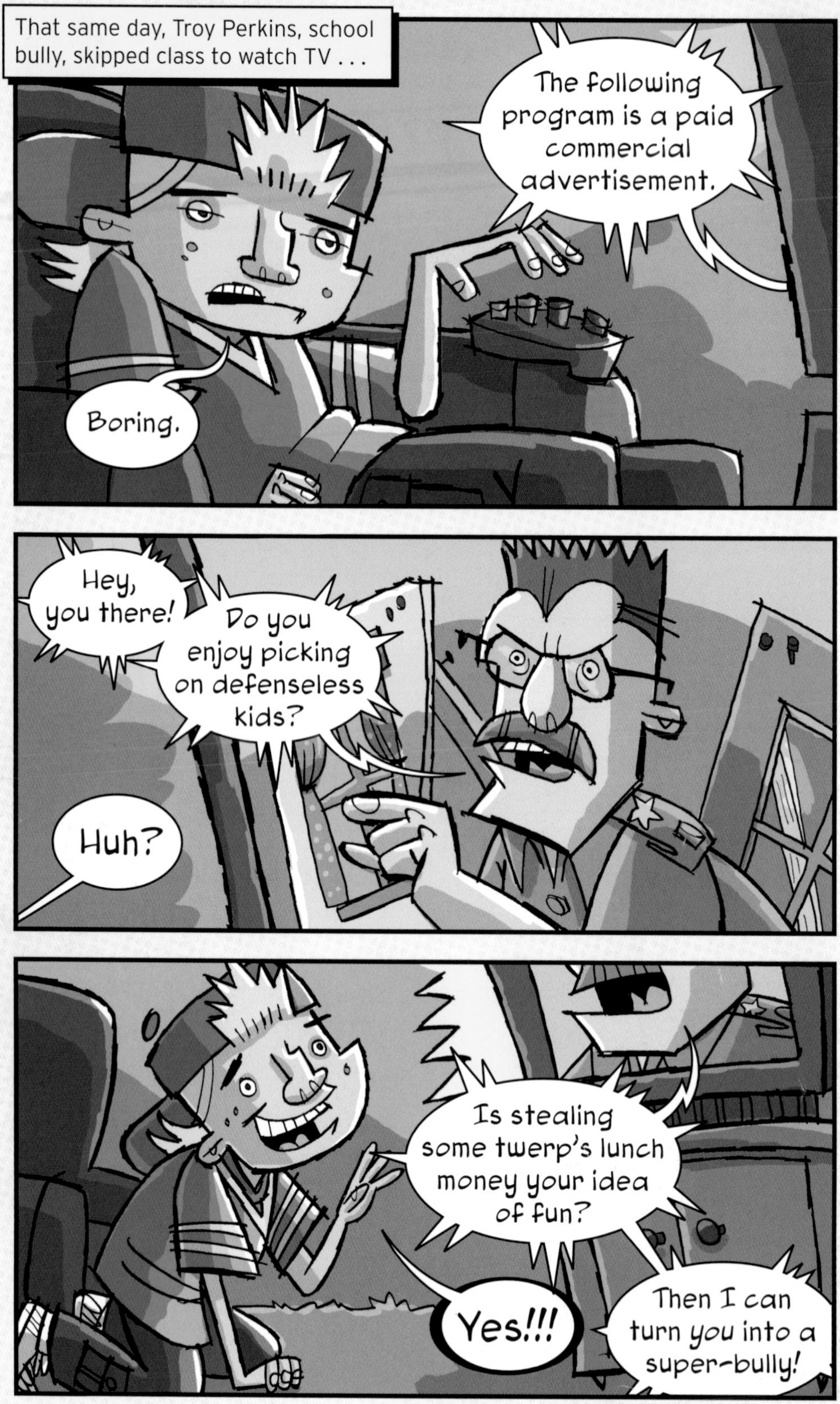
That same day, Troy Perkins, school bully, skipped class to watch TV . . .
The following program is a paid commercial advertisement.
Boring.
Hey, you there!
Do you enjoy picking on defenseless kids?
Huh?
Is stealing some twerp's lunch money your idea of fun?
Yes!!!
Then I can turn *you* into a super-bully!

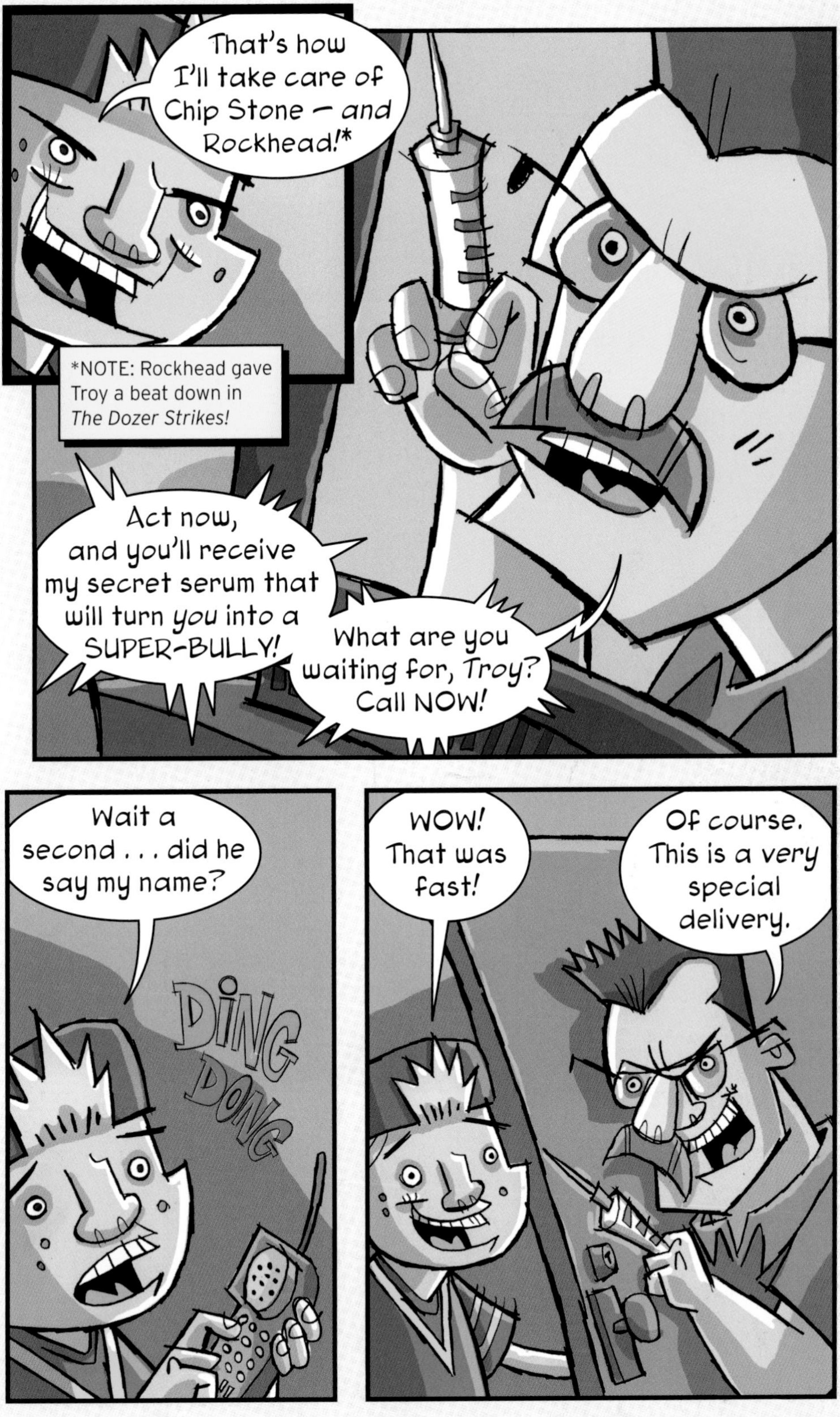
That's how I'll take care of Chip Stone — and Rockhead!*
*NOTE: Rockhead gave Troy a beat down in *The Dozer Strikes!*
Act now, and you'll receive my secret serum that will turn *you* into a SUPER-BULLY!
What are you waiting for, Troy? Call NOW!
Wait a second . . . did he say my name?
DING DONG
WOW! That was fast!
Of course. This is a very special delivery.

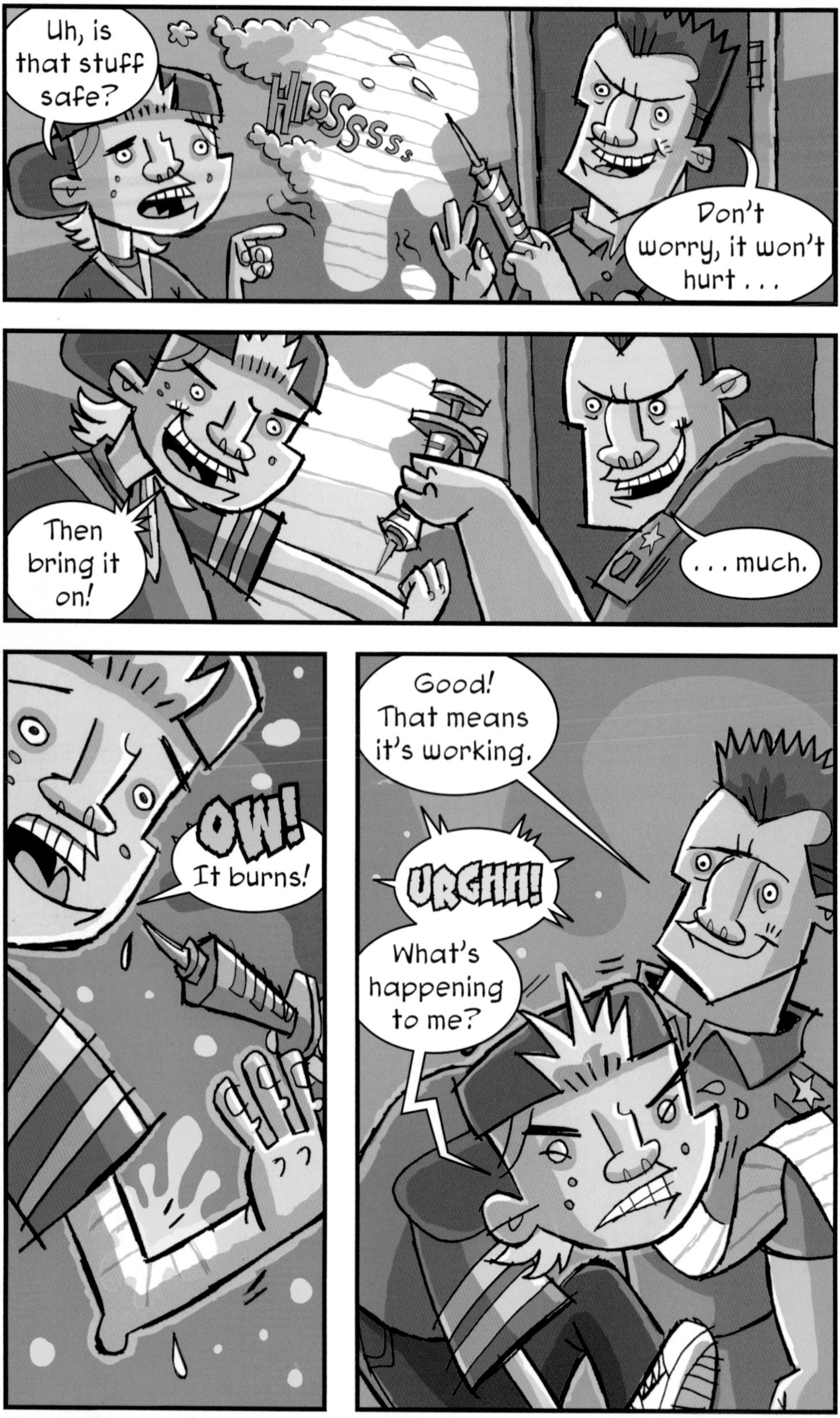

Uh, is that stuff safe?
HISSSSSs
Don't worry, it won't hurt . . .
Then bring it on!
. . . much.
OW! It burns!
Good! That means it's working.
URGHH!
What's happening to me?

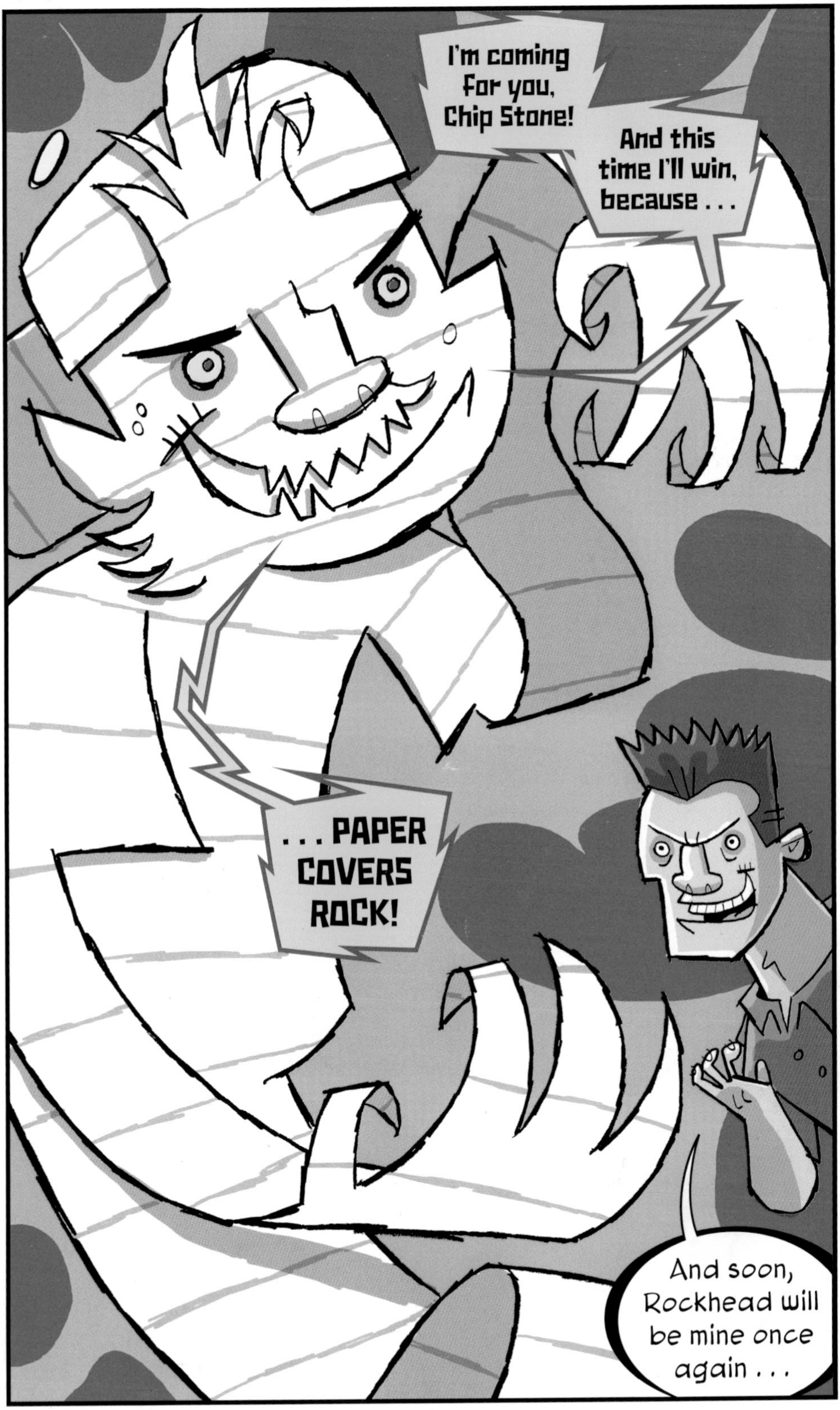
I'm coming for you, Chip Stone!
And this time I'll win, because . . .
. . . PAPER COVERS ROCK!
And soon, Rockhead will be mine once again . . .

Huh.
Where'd that salesman go?
RUSTLE RUSTLE
Oh well. Time to try out my new superpowers!
Look out, Banner Elementary!
Here comes PAPERCUT!
WHOOSH

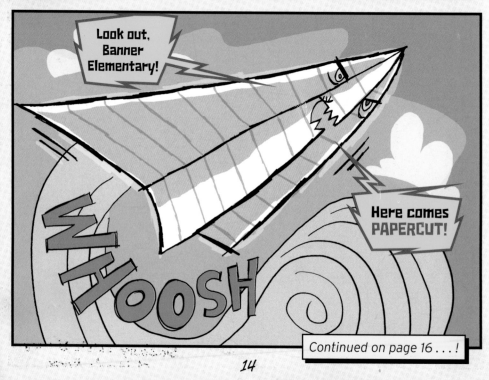

Continued on page 16 . . . !

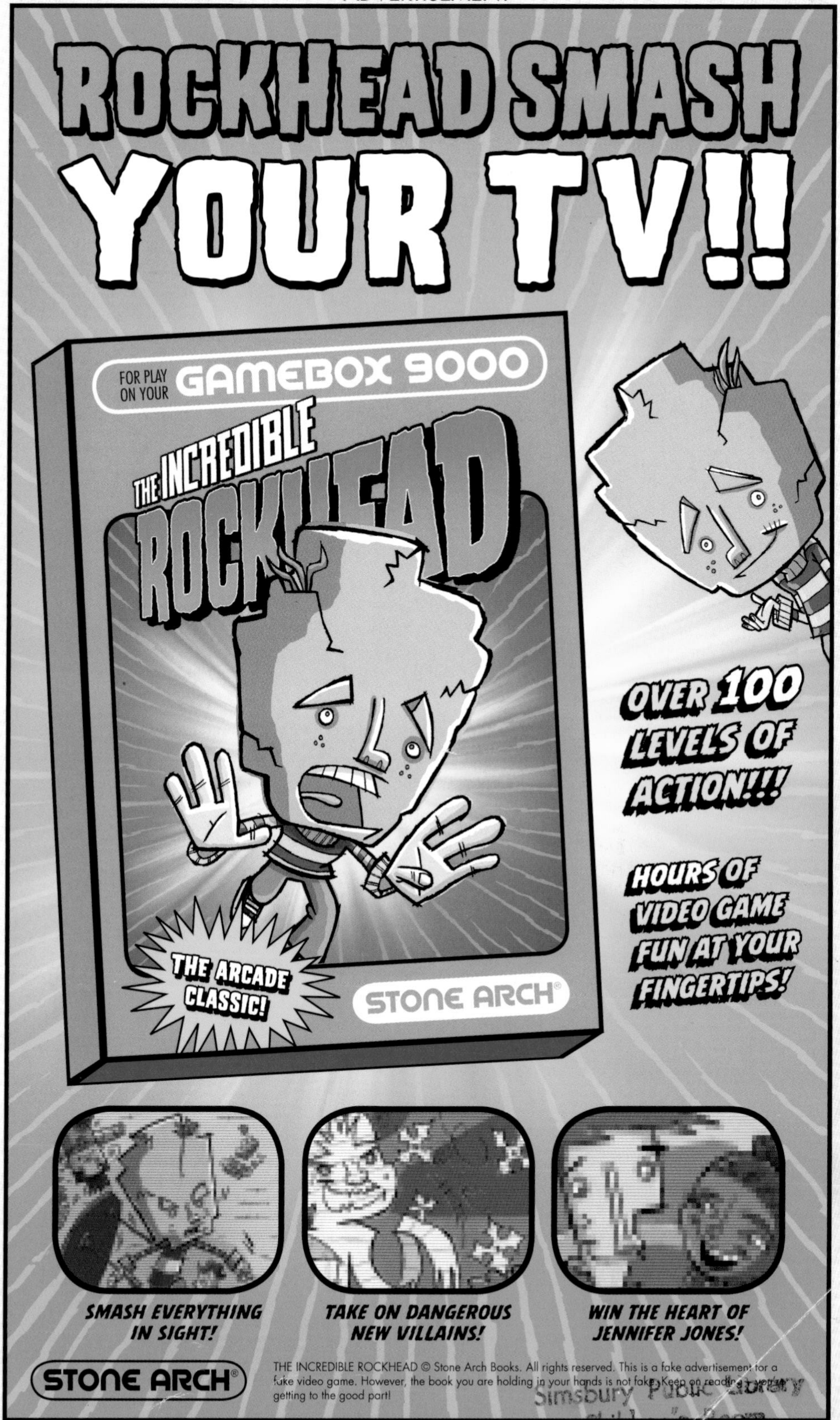
ROCKHEAD SMASH
YOUR TV!!
FOR PLAY ON YOUR GAMEBOX 9000
THE INCREDIBLE ROCKHEAD
THE ARCADE CLASSIC!
STONE ARCH®
OVER 100 LEVELS OF ACTION!!!
HOURS OF VIDEO GAME FUN AT YOUR FINGERTIPS!
SMASH EVERYTHING IN SIGHT!
TAKE ON DANGEROUS NEW VILLAINS!
WIN THE HEART OF JENNIFER JONES!
STONE ARCH®
THE INCREDIBLE ROCKHEAD © Stone Arch Books. All rights reserved. This is a fake advertisement for a fake video game. However, the book you are holding in your hands is not fake. Keep on reading — you're getting to the good part!

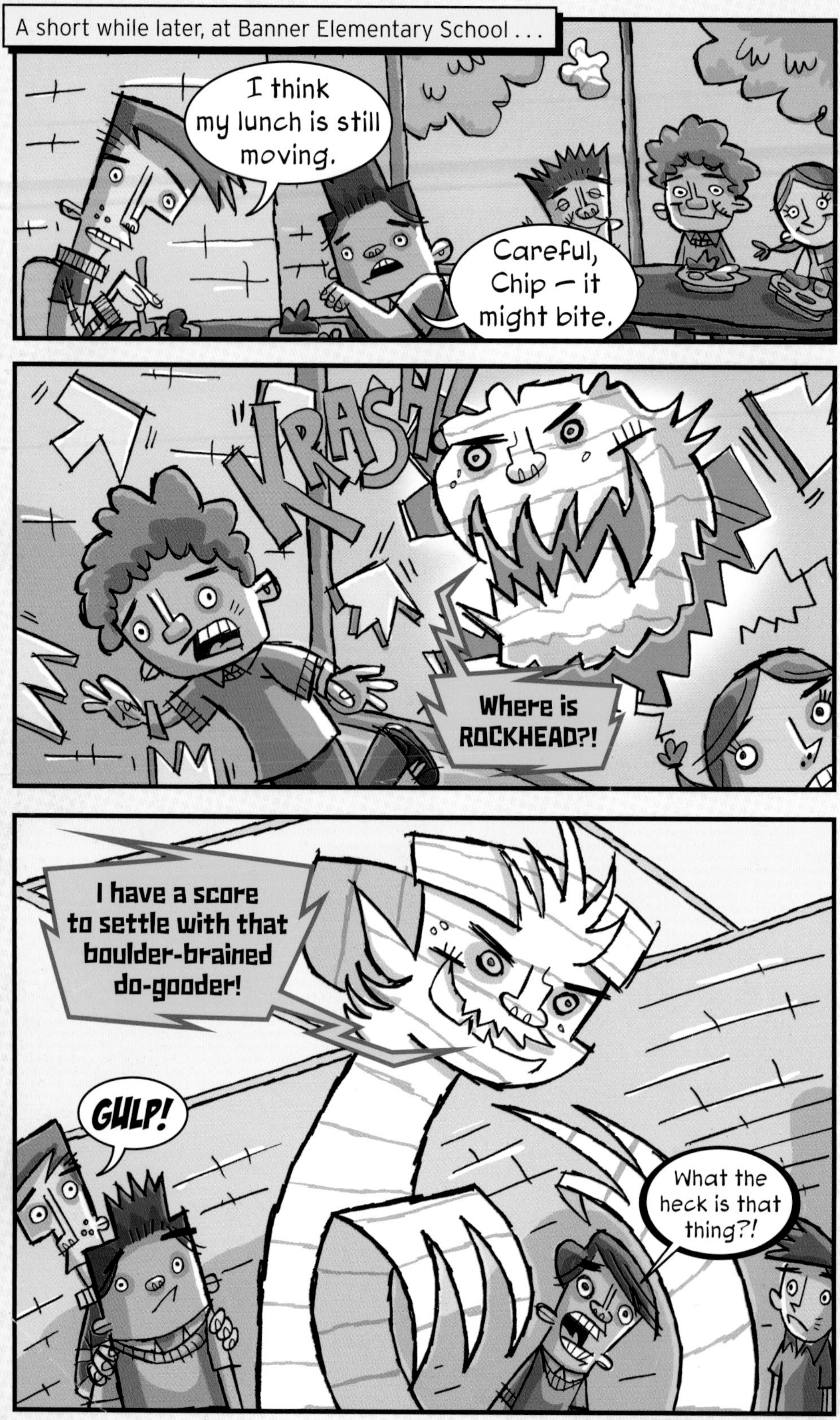
A short while later, at Banner Elementary School . . .
I think my lunch is still moving.
Careful, Chip — it might bite.
KRASH!
Where is ROCKHEAD?!
I have a score to settle with that boulder-brained do-gooder!
GULP!
What the heck is that thing?!

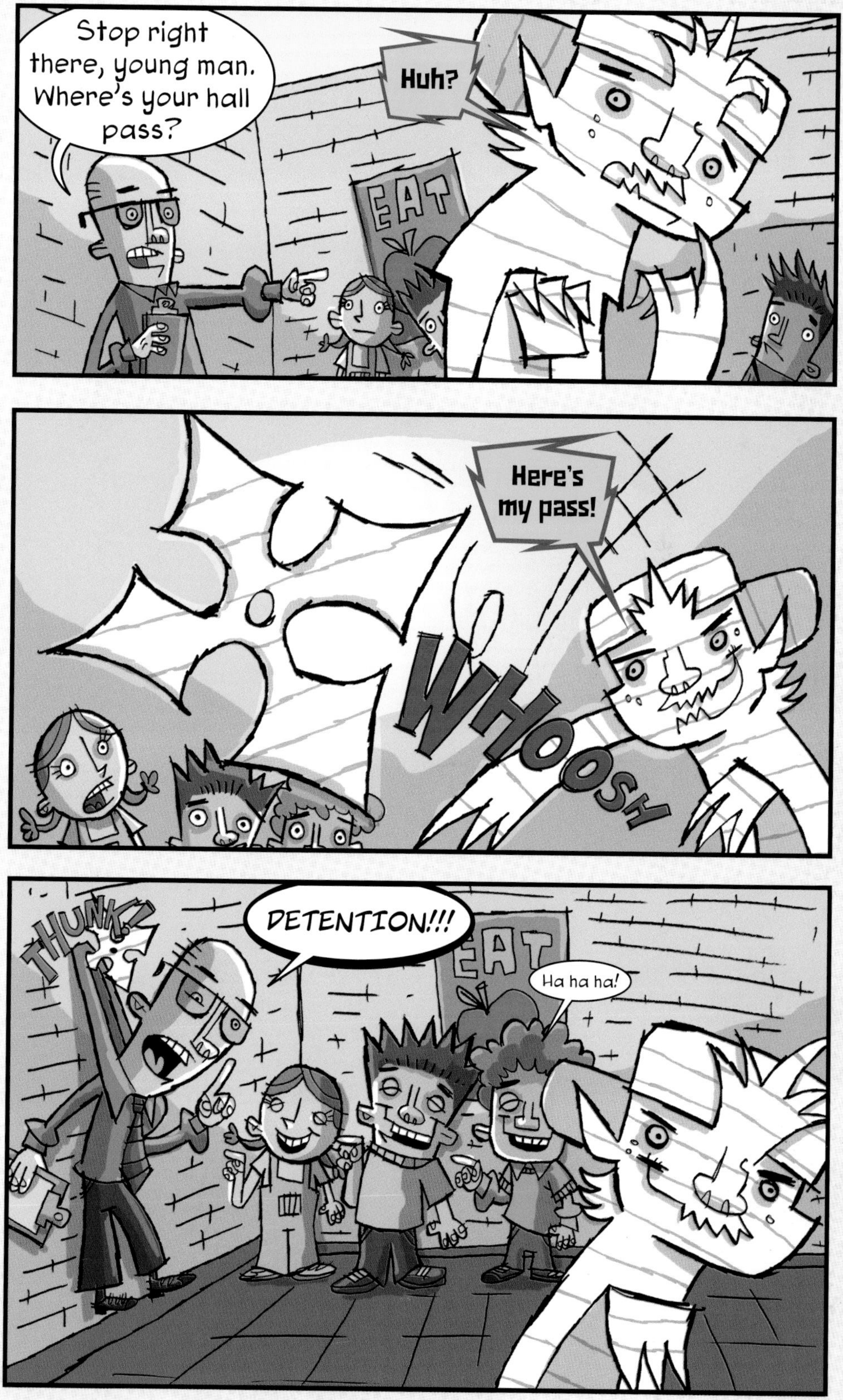
Stop right there, young man. Where's your hall pass?
Huh?
EAT
Here's my pass!
WHOOSH
THUNK!
DETENTION!!!
EAT
Ha ha ha!

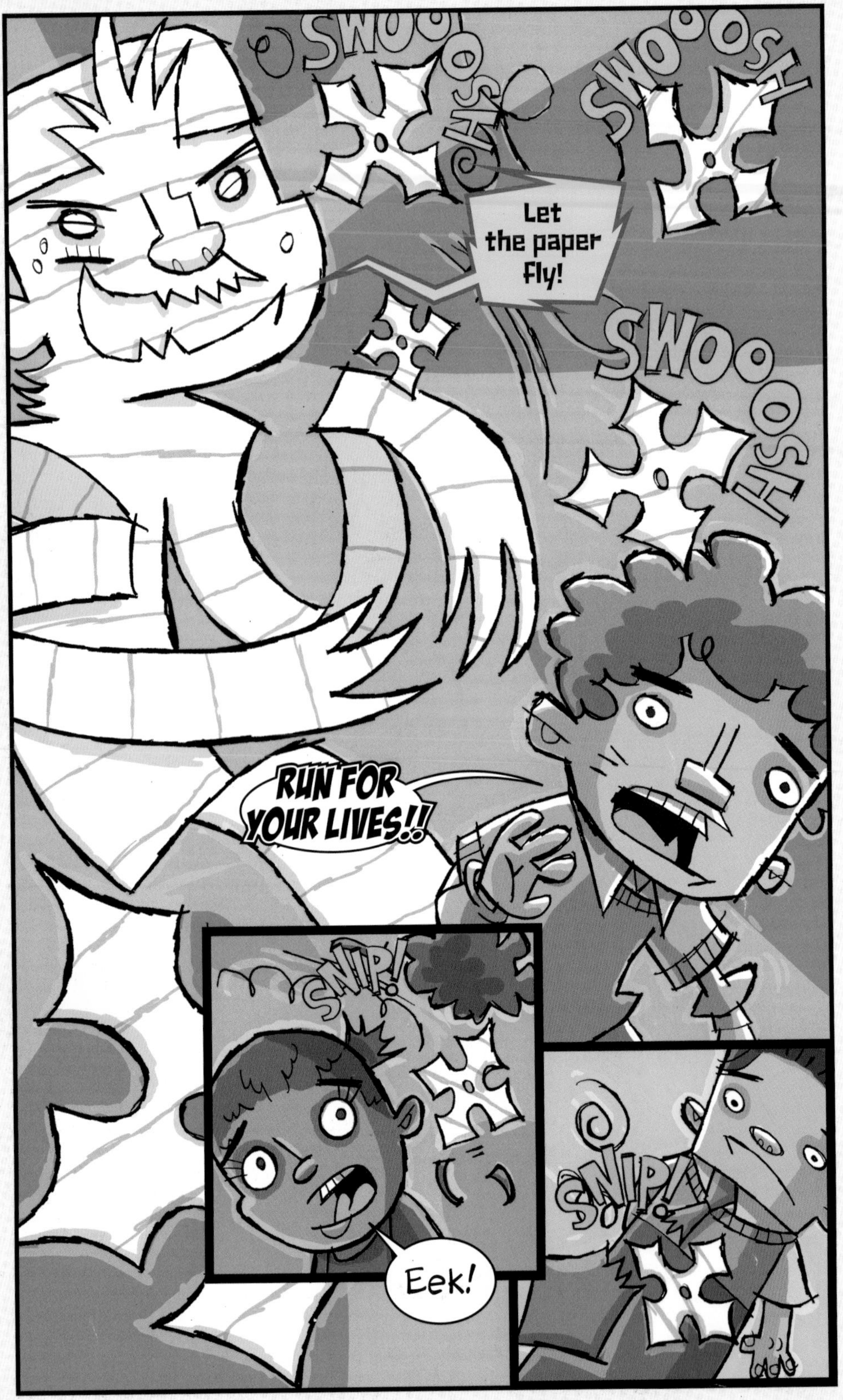
SWOOOSH
SWOOOSH
Let the paper fly!
SWOOOSH
RUN FOR YOUR LIVES!!
SNIP!
Eek!
SNIP!

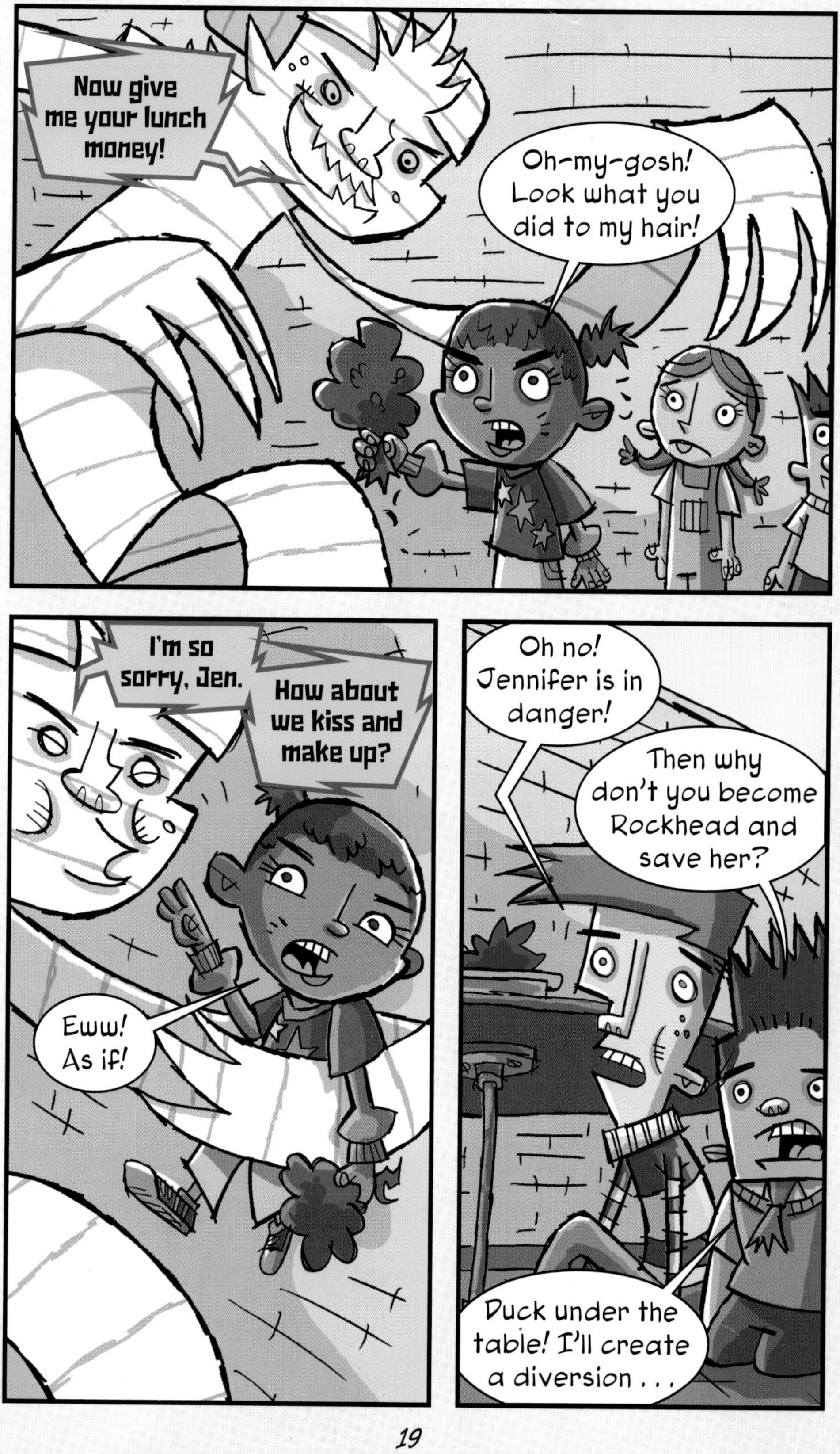
Now give me your lunch money!
Oh-my-gosh! Look what you did to my hair!
I'm so sorry, Jen.
How about we kiss and make up?
Eww! As if!
Oh no! Jennifer is in danger!
Then why don't you become Rockhead and save her?
Duck under the table! I'll create a diversion . . .

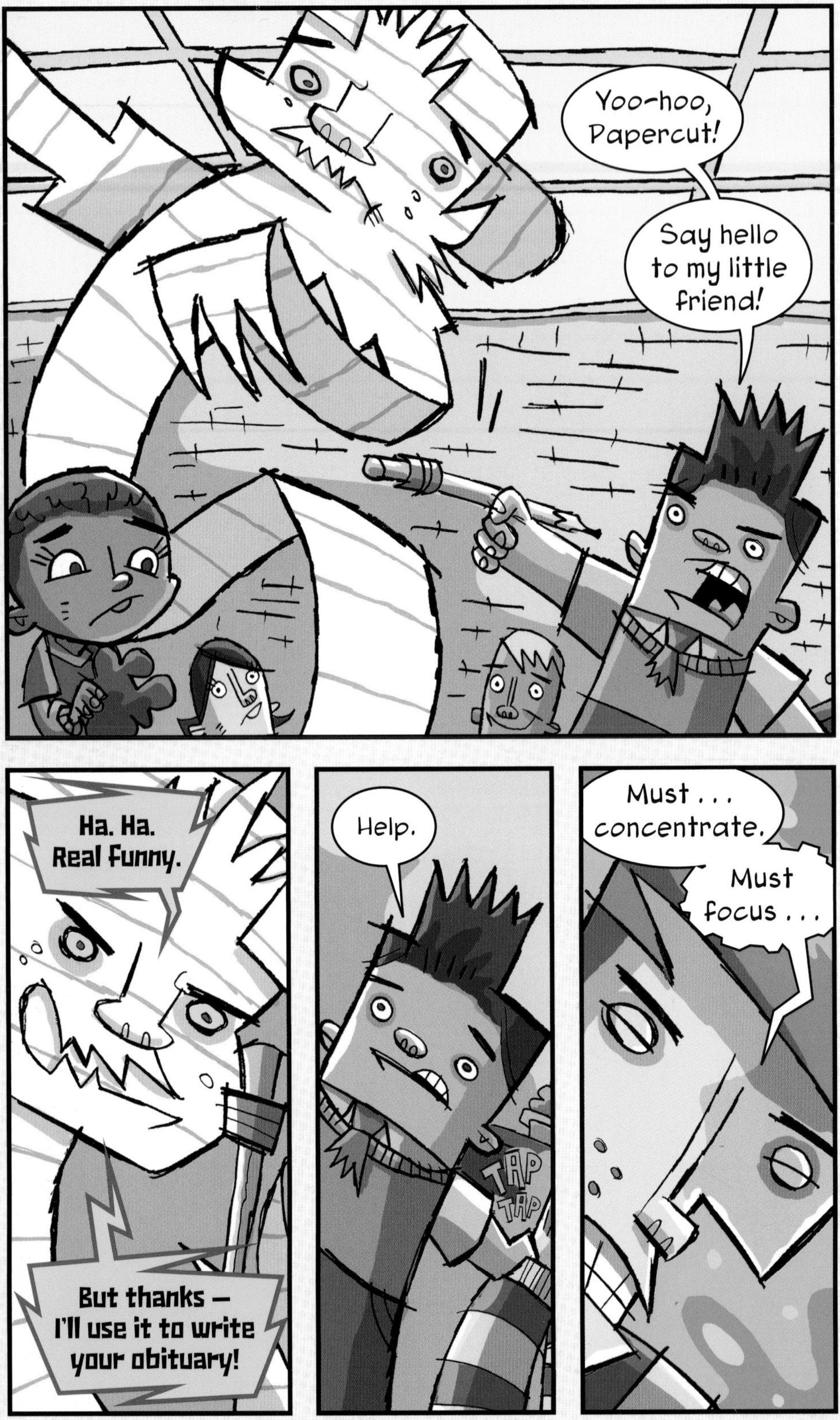

Yoo-hoo, Papercut!
Say hello to my little friend!
Ha. Ha. Real funny.
But thanks — I'll use it to write your obituary!
Help.
TAP TAP
Must . . . concentrate.
Must focus . . .

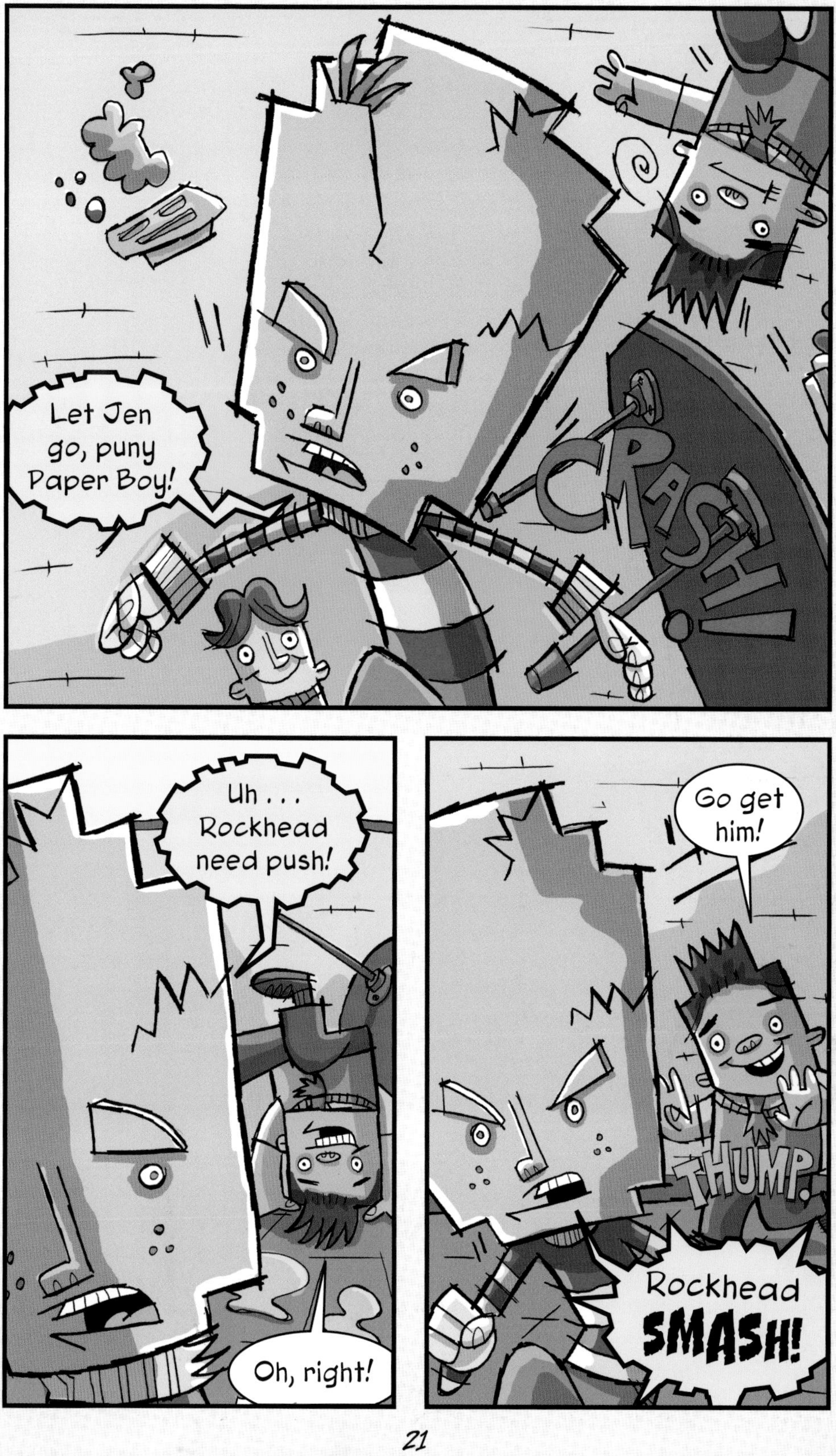
Let Jen go, puny Paper Boy!
CRASH!
Uh . . . Rockhead need push!
Oh, right!
Go get him!
THUMP.
Rockhead SMASH!

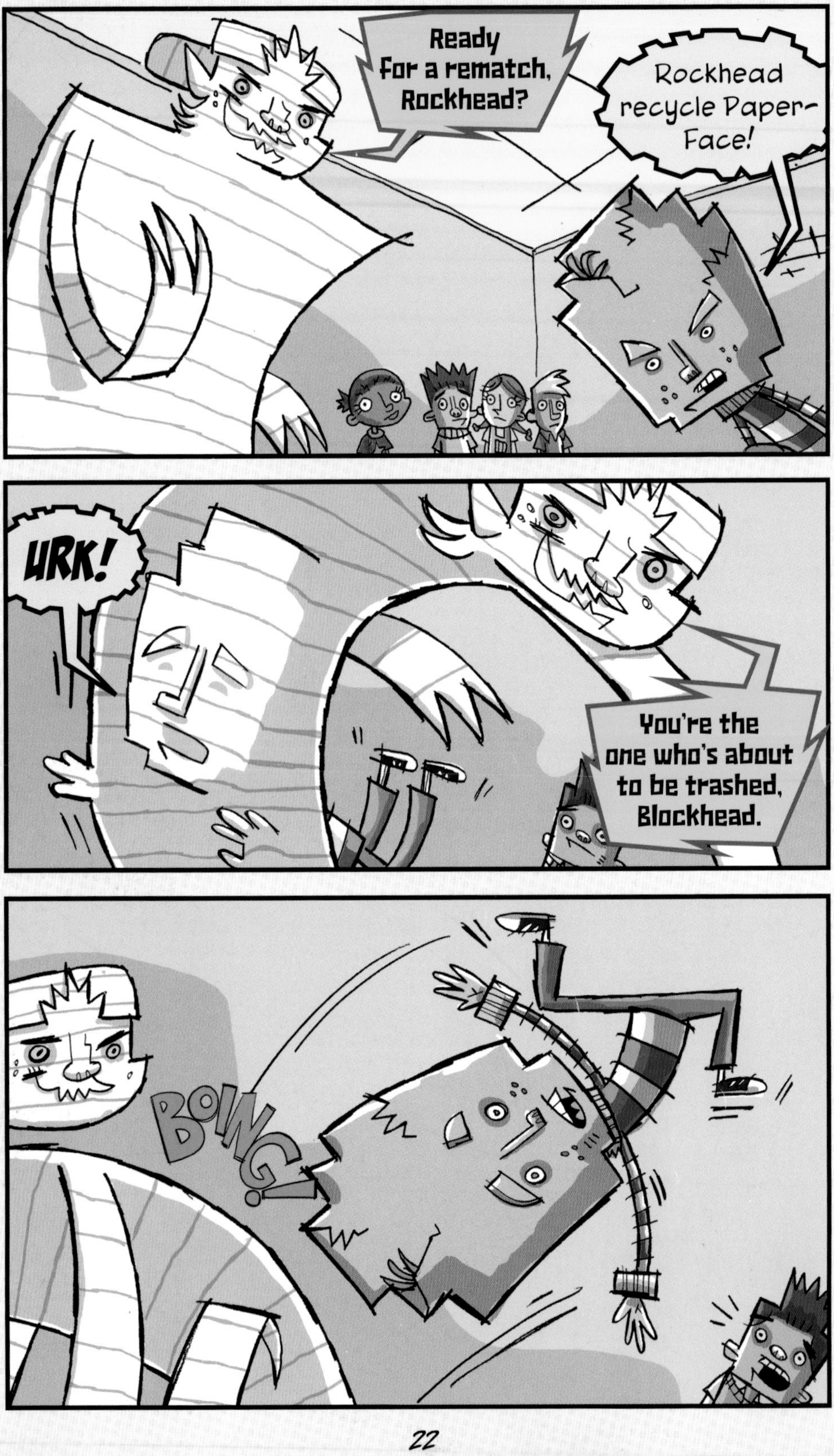

Ready for a rematch, Rockhead?
Rockhead recycle Paper-Face!
URK!
You're the one who's about to be trashed, Blockhead.
BOING!

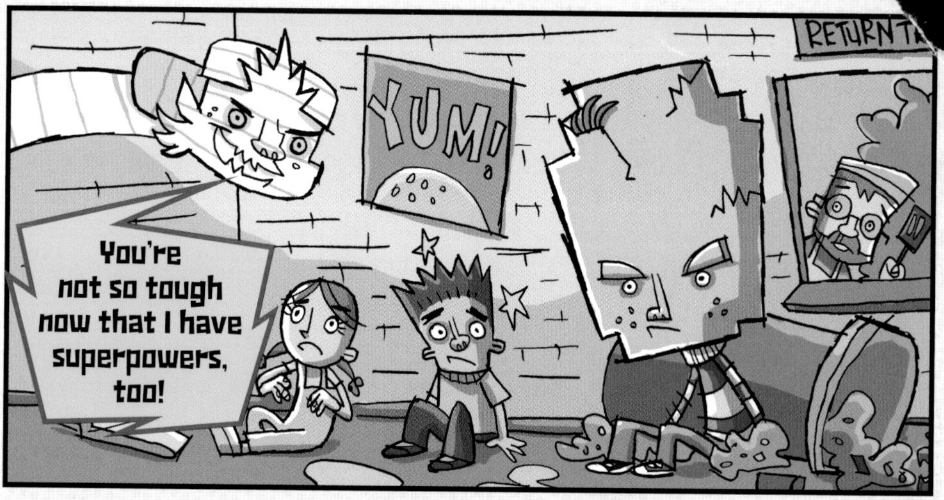
RETURN T
YUM!
You're not so tough now that I have superpowers, too!

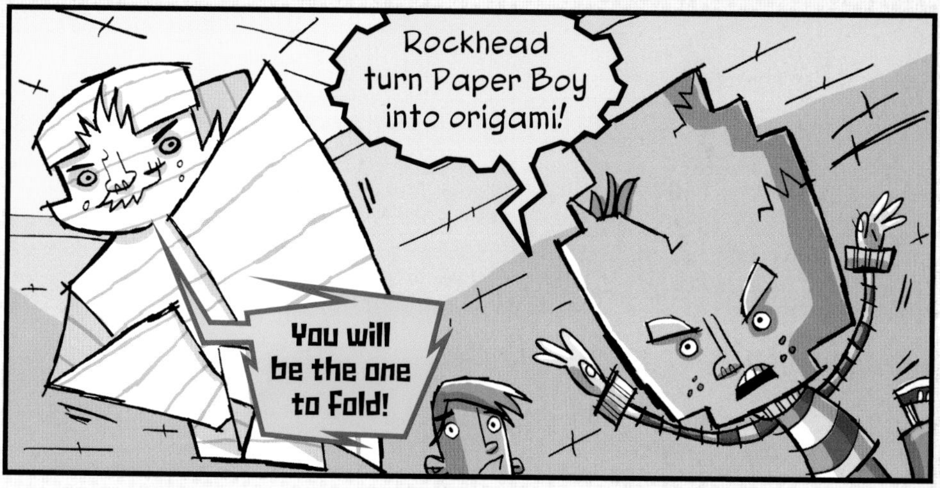
Rockhead turn Paper Boy into origami!
You will be the one to fold!

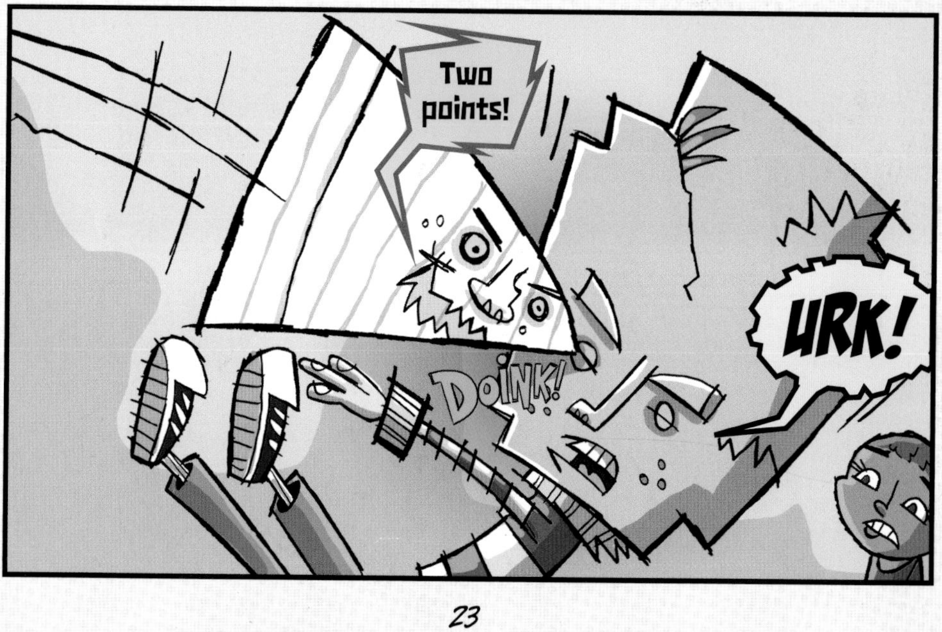
Two points!
DOINK!
URK!

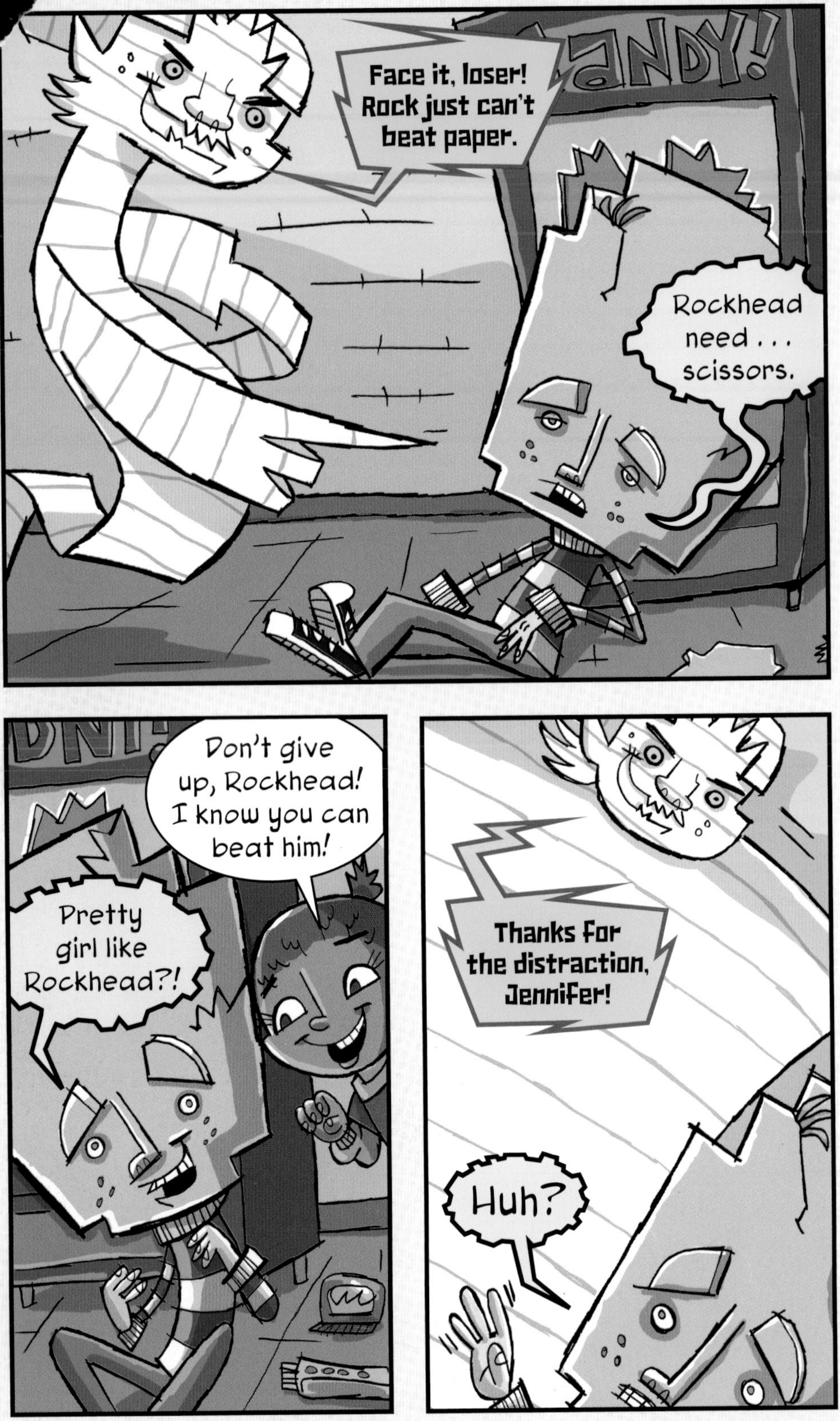
ANDY!
Face it, loser! Rock just can't beat paper.
Rockhead need . . . scissors.
Don't give up, Rockhead! I know you can beat him!
Pretty girl like Rockhead?!
Thanks for the distraction, Jennifer!
Huh?

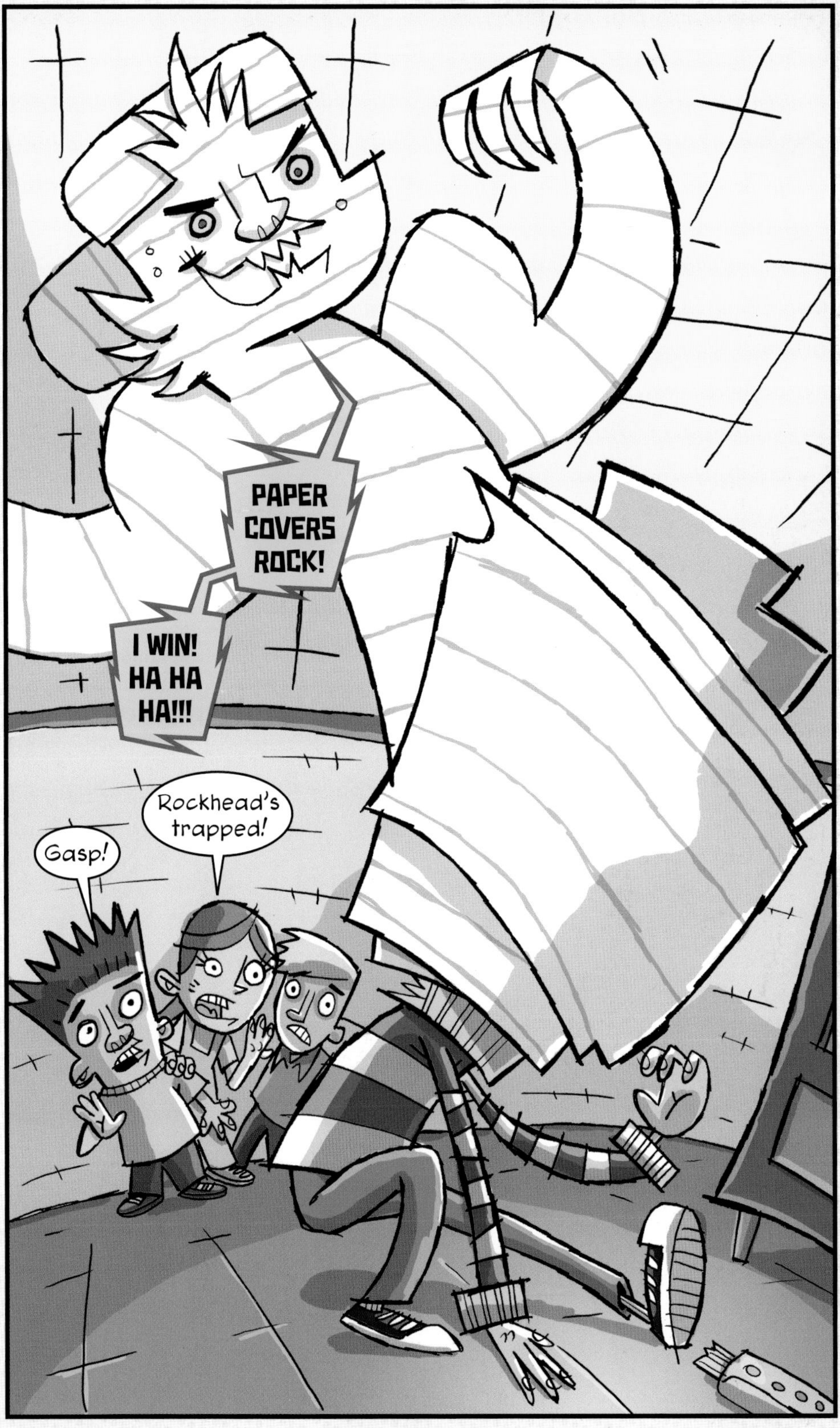
PAPER COVERS ROCK!
I WIN! HA HA HA!!!
Rockhead's trapped!
Gasp!

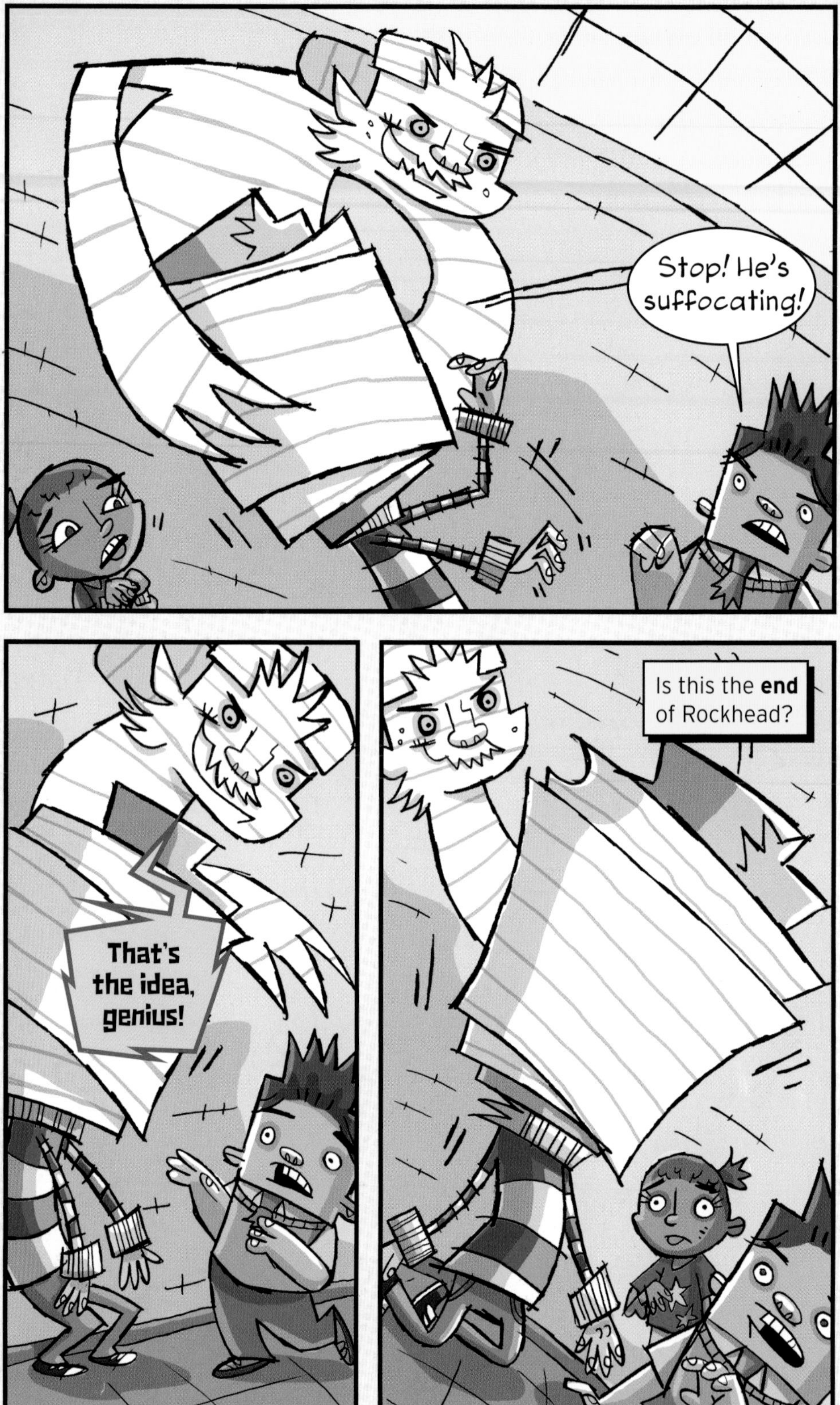
Stop! He's suffocating!
That's the idea, genius!
Is this the **end** of Rockhead?

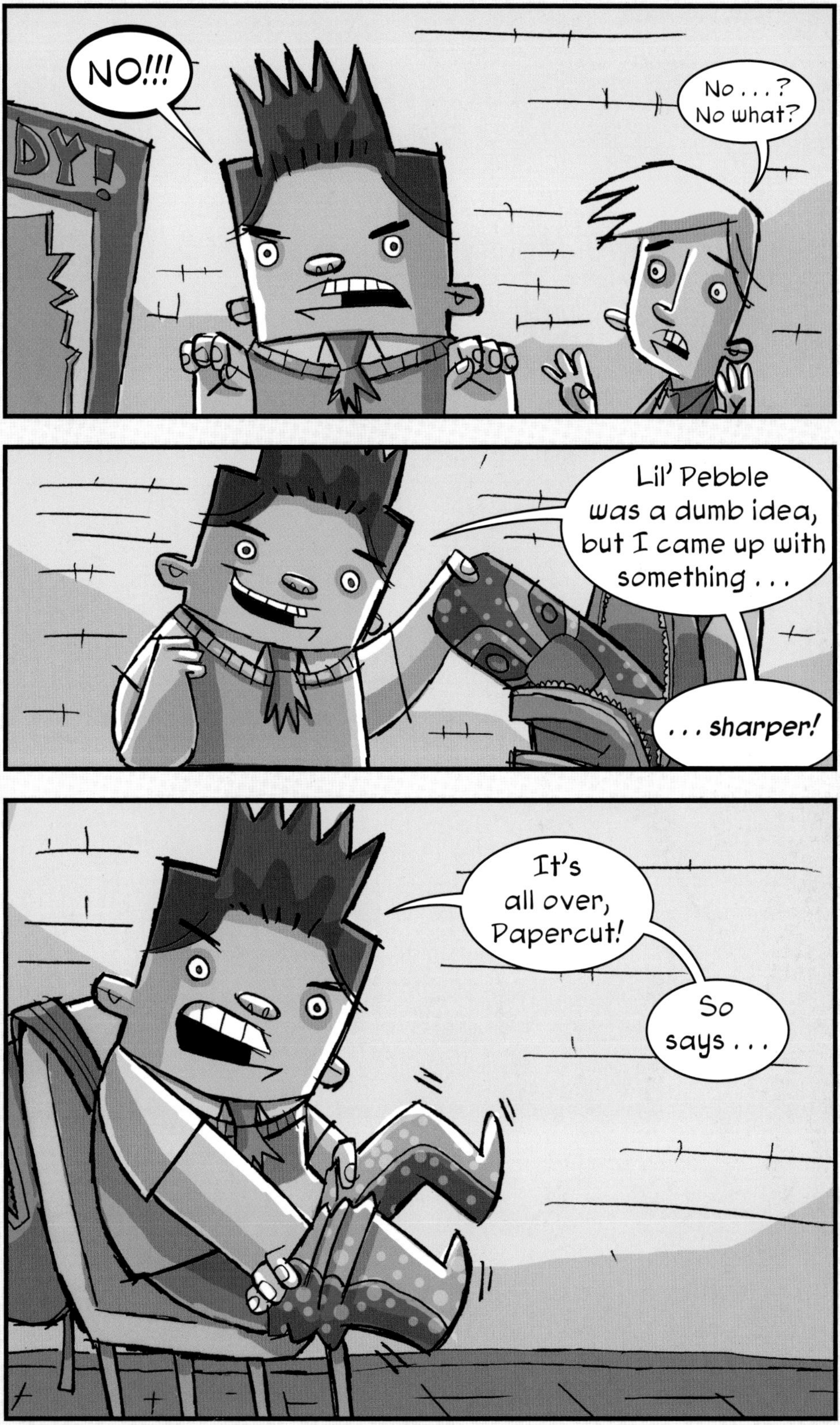

NO!!!
No . . . ? No what?
Lil' Pebble was a dumb idea, but I came up with something . . .
. . . sharper!
It's all over, Papercut!
So says . . .

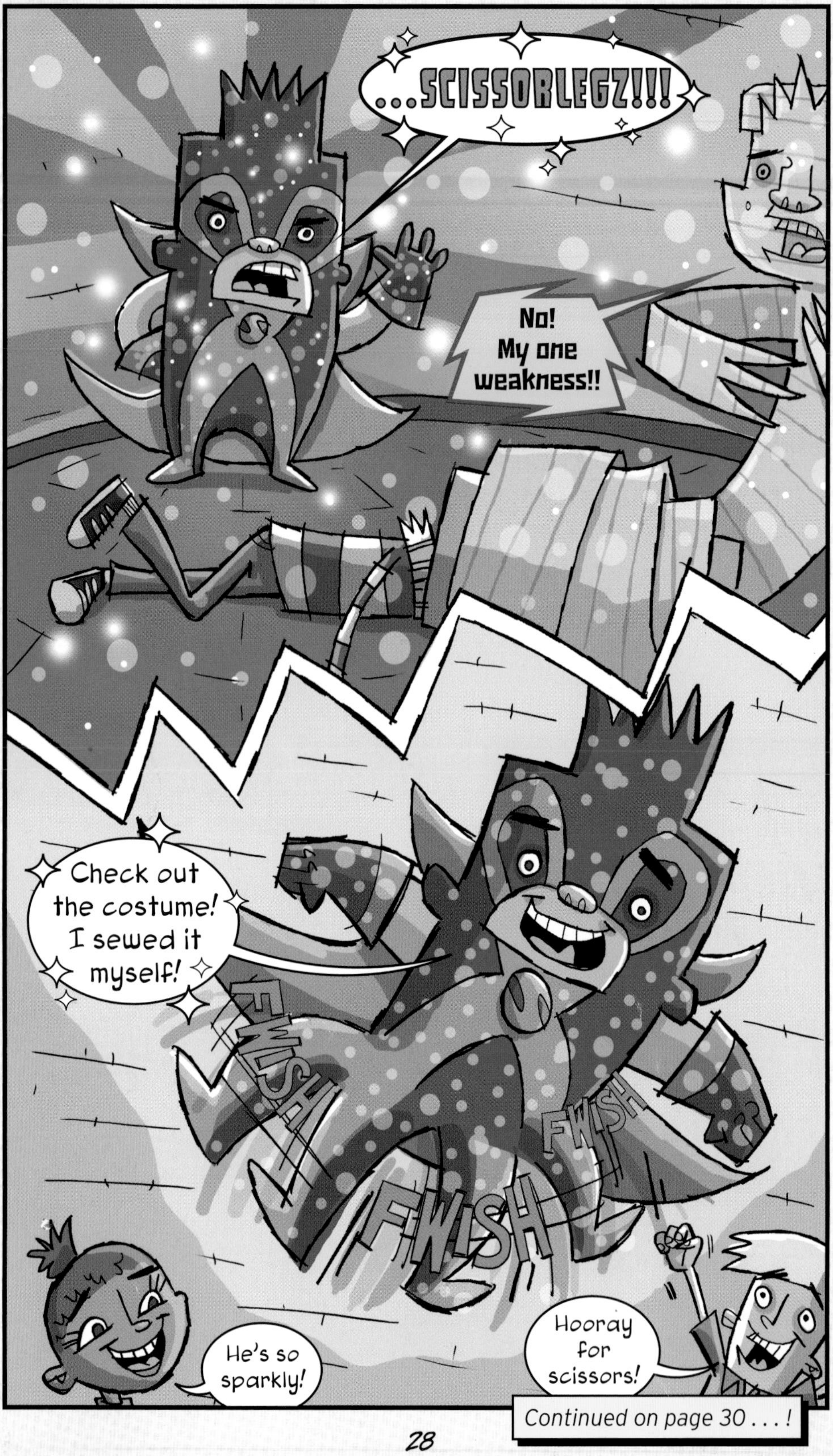
...SCISSORLEGZ!!!
No! My one weakness!!
Check out the costume! I sewed it myself!
FWISH
FWISH
FWISH
He's so sparkly!
Hooray for scissors!

Continued on page 30 . . . !

ADVERTISEMENT

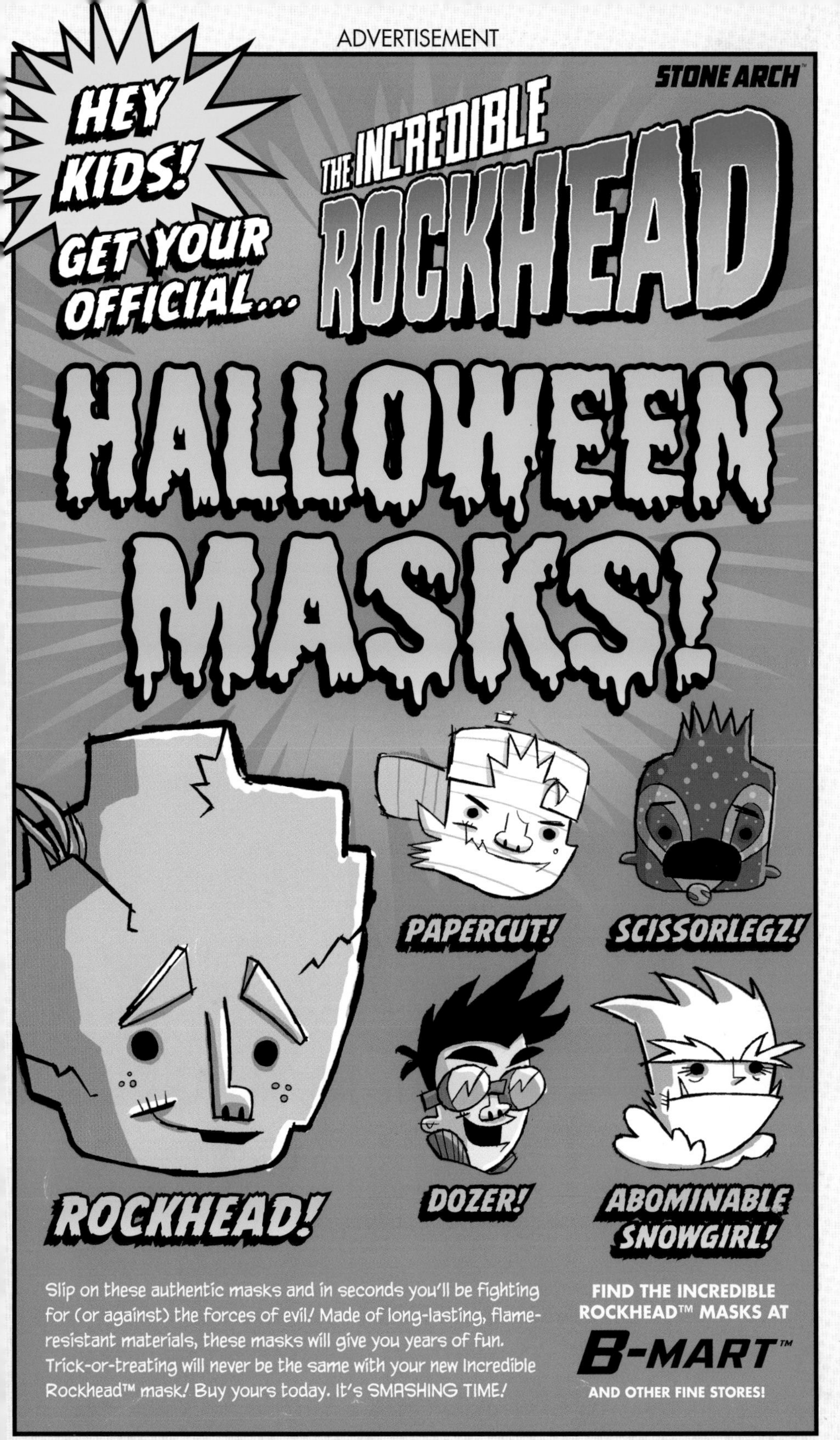

STONE ARCH
HEY KIDS!
GET YOUR OFFICIAL...
THE INCREDIBLE ROCKHEAD
HALLOWEEN MASKS!
PAPERCUT!
SCISSORLEGZ!
ROCKHEAD!
DOZER!
ABOMINABLE SNOWGIRL!
Slip on these authentic masks and in seconds you'll be fighting for (or against) the forces of evil! Made of long-lasting, flame-resistant materials, these masks will give you years of fun. Trick-or-treating will never be the same with your new Incredible Rockhead™ mask! Buy yours today. It's SMASHING TIME!
FIND THE INCREDIBLE ROCKHEAD™ MASKS AT
B-MART™
AND OTHER FINE STORES!

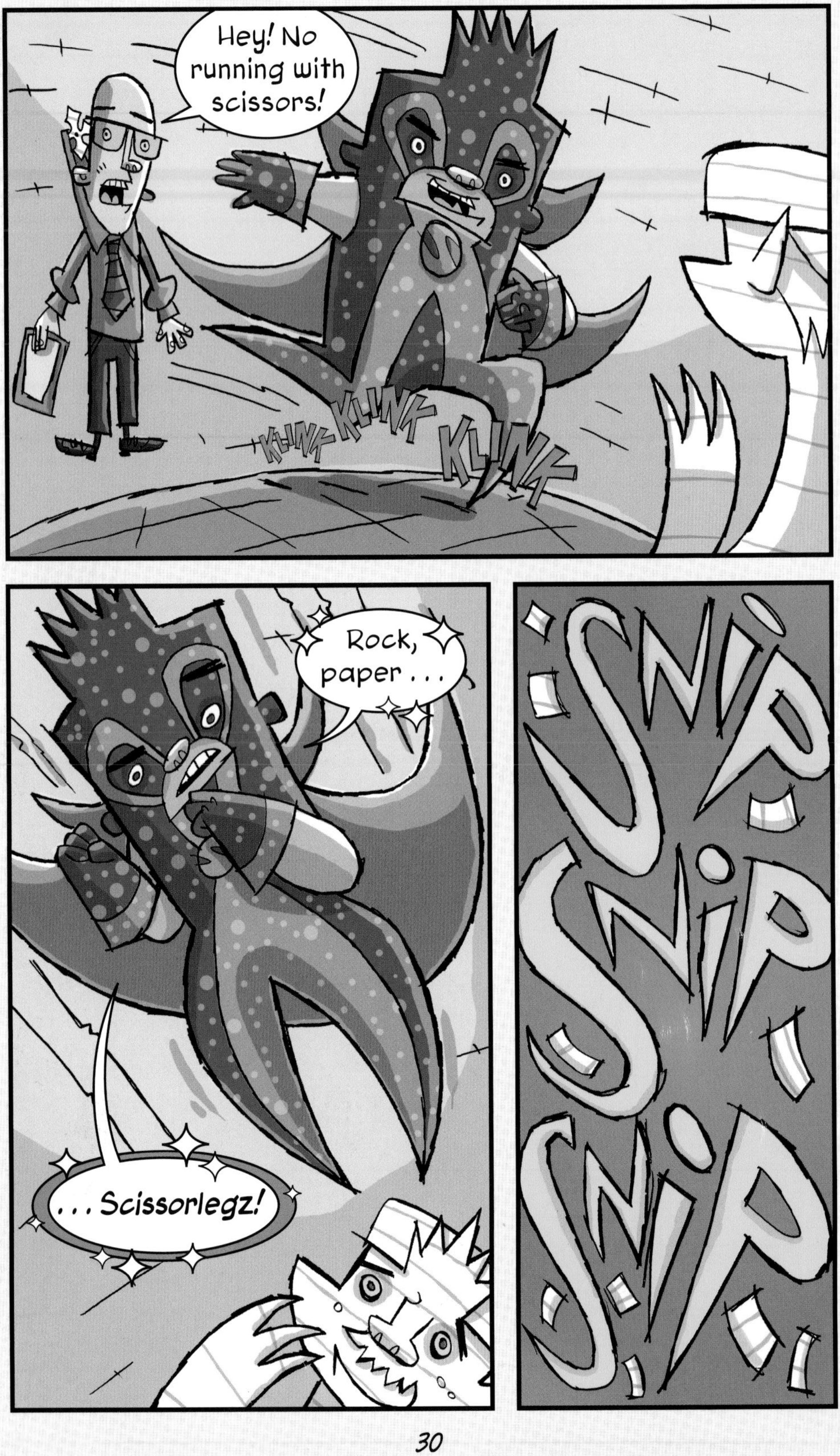
Hey! No running with scissors!
KLINK KLINK KLINK
Rock, paper . . .
. . . Scissorlegz!
SNIP SNIP SNIP

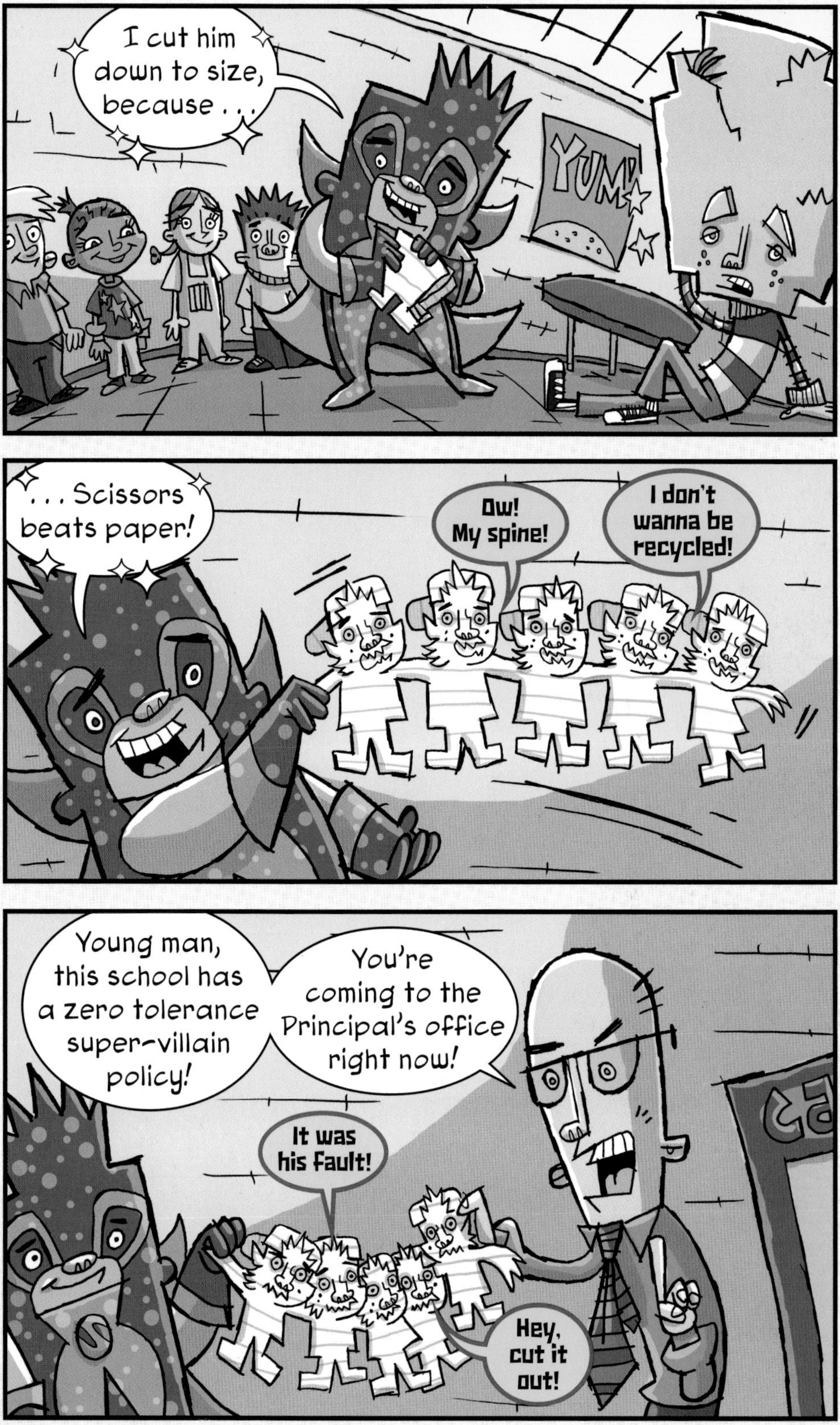
I cut him down to size, because . . .
YUM!
. . . Scissors beats paper!
Ow! My spine!
I don't wanna be recycled!
Young man, this school has a zero tolerance super-villain policy!
You're coming to the Principal's office right now!
It was his fault!
Hey, cut it out!

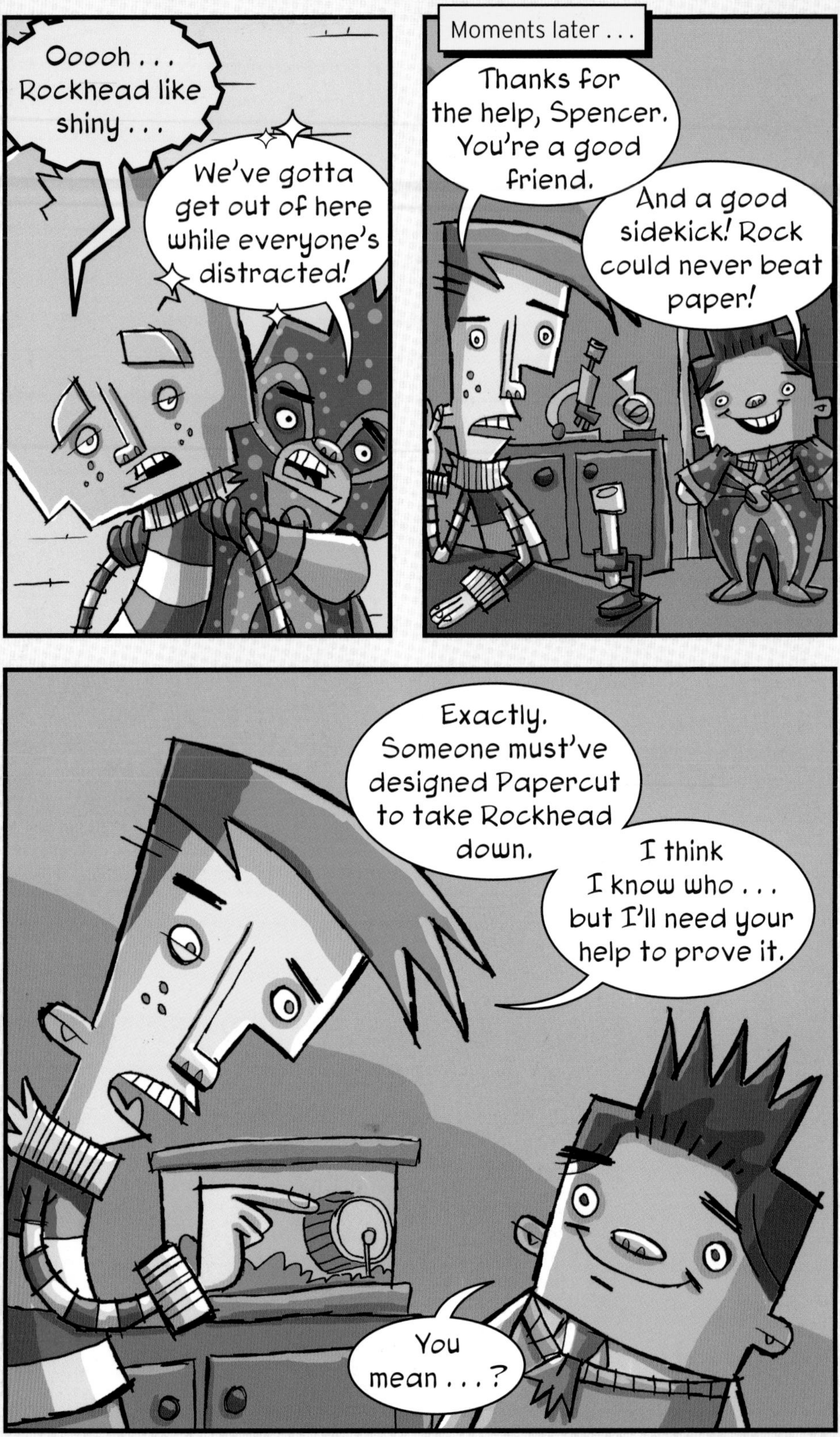
Ooooh . . . Rockhead like shiny . . .
We've gotta get out of here while everyone's distracted!
Moments later . . .
Thanks for the help, Spencer. You're a good friend.
And a good sidekick! Rock could never beat paper!
Exactly. Someone must've designed Papercut to take Rockhead down.
I think I know who . . . but I'll need your help to prove it.
You mean . . . ?

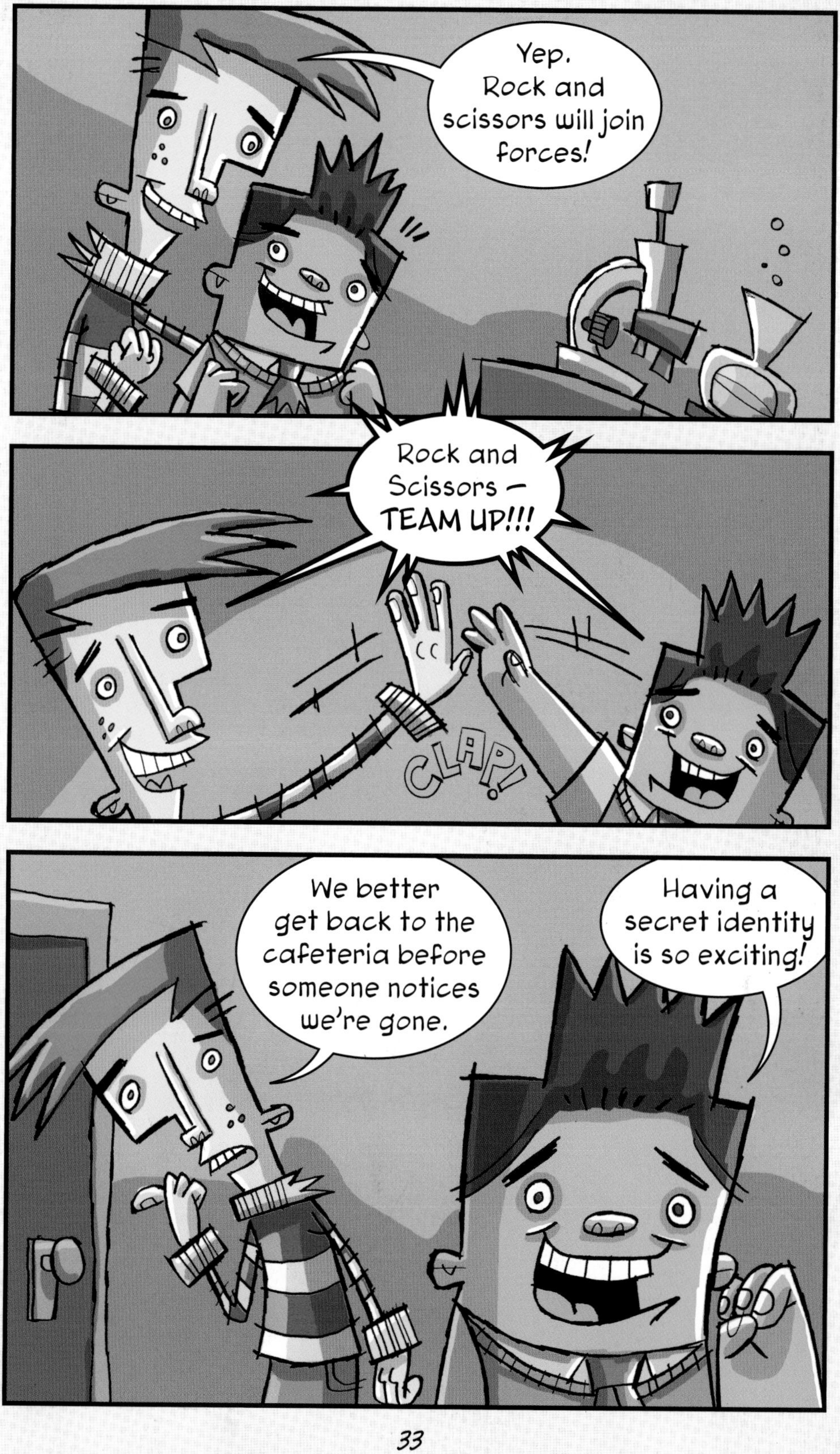
Yep.
Rock and scissors will join forces!
Rock and Scissors — TEAM UP!!!
CLAP!
We better get back to the cafeteria before someone notices we're gone.
Having a secret identity is so exciting!

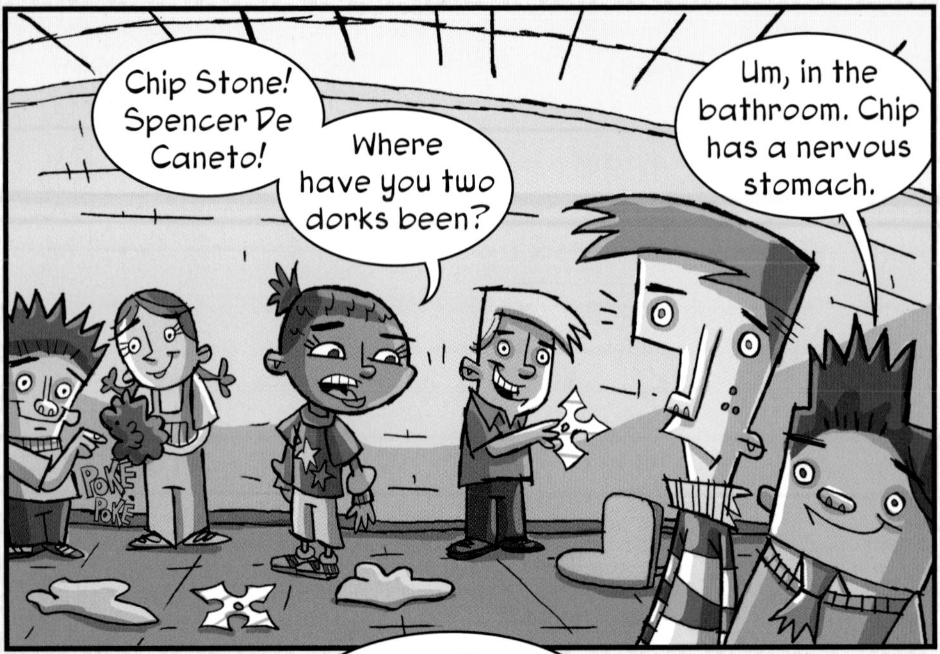
Chip Stone! Spencer De Caneto!
Where have you two dorks been?
Um, in the bathroom. Chip has a nervous stomach.
POKE POKE

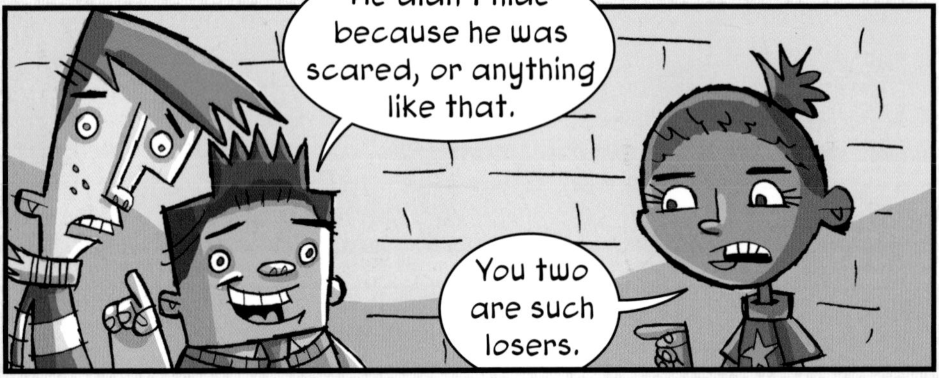
He didn't hide because he was scared, or anything like that.
You two are such losers.

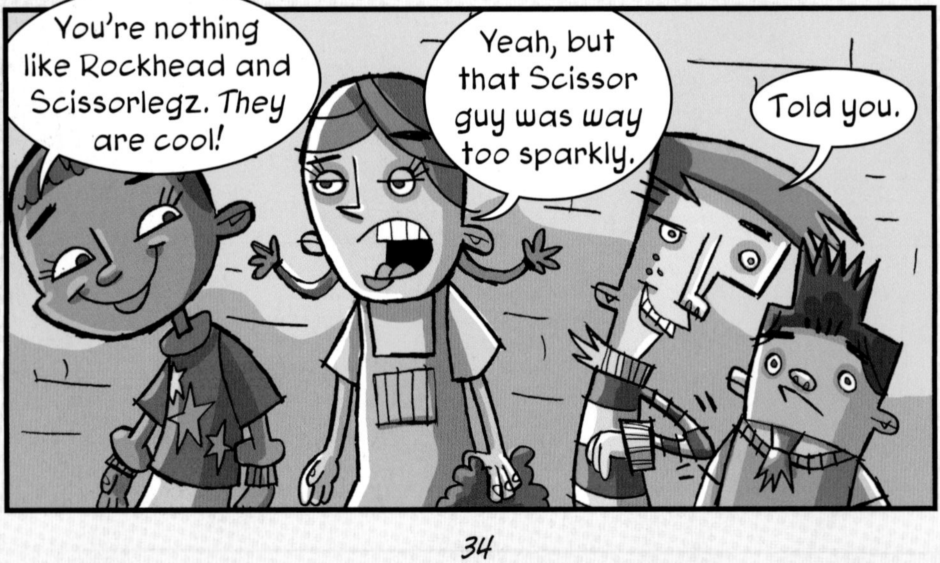
You're nothing like Rockhead and Scissorlegz. They are cool!
Yeah, but that Scissor guy was way too sparkly.
Told you.

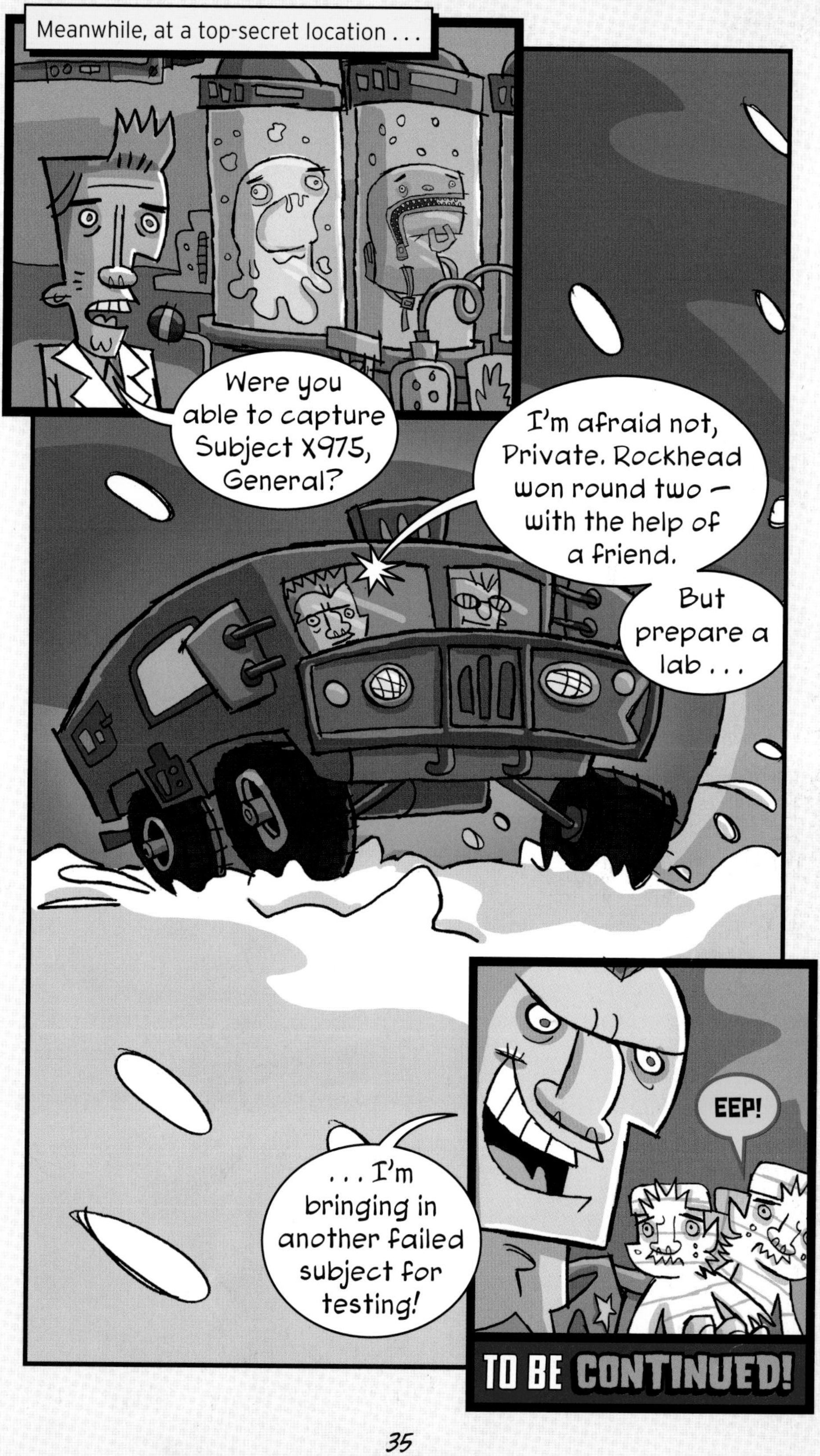
Meanwhile, at a top-secret location . . .
Were you able to capture Subject X975, General?
I'm afraid not, Private. Rockhead won round two — with the help of a friend.
But prepare a lab . . .
. . . I'm bringing in another failed subject for testing!
EEP!
TO BE CONTINUED!

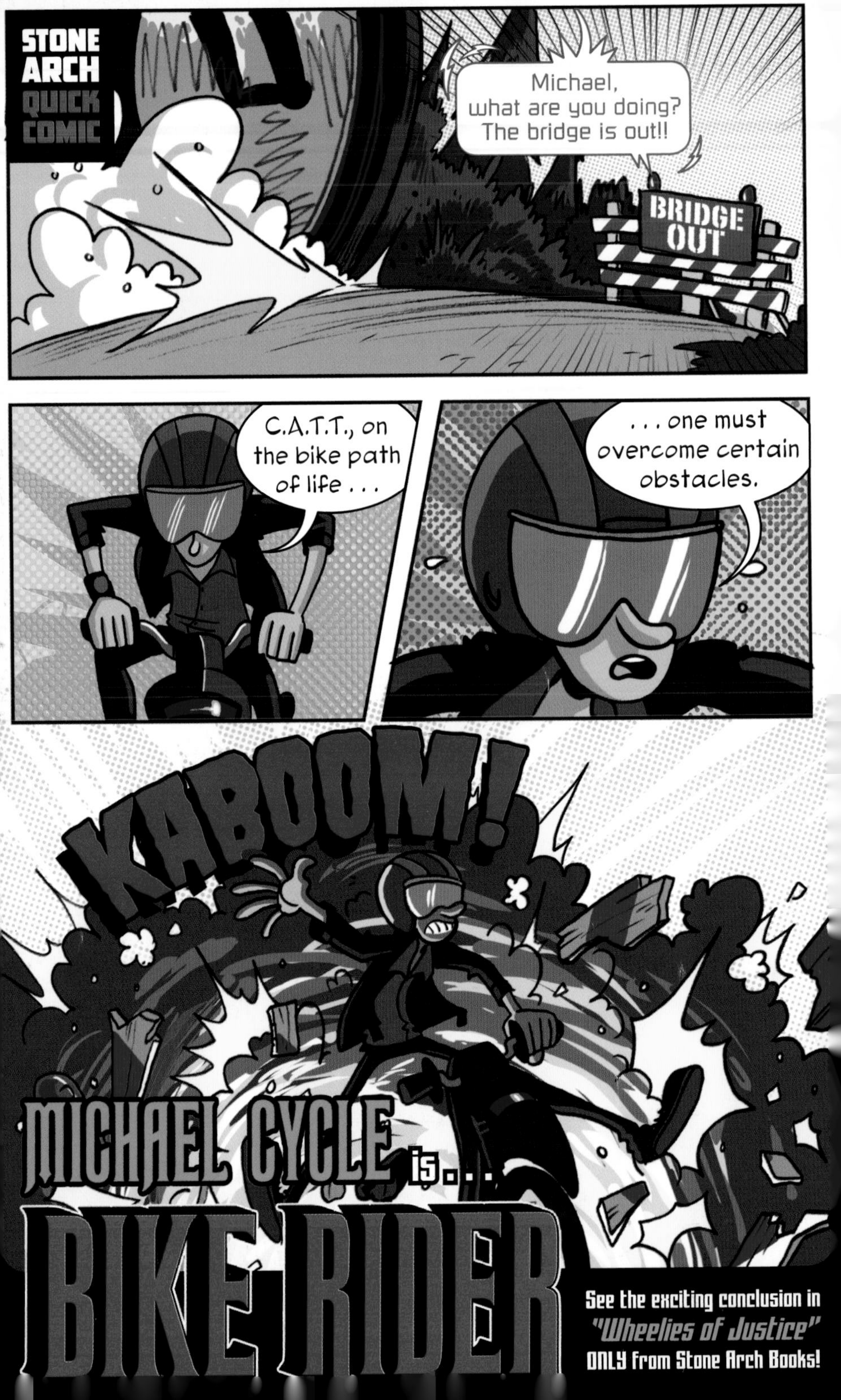
STONE ARCH QUICK COMIC
Michael, what are you doing? The bridge is out!!
BRIDGE OUT
C.A.T.T., on the bike path of life . . .
. . . one must overcome certain obstacles.
KABOOM!
MICHAEL CYCLE is . . .
BIKE RIDER
See the exciting conclusion in "Wheelies of Justice" ONLY from Stone Arch Books!

FROM THE DESK OF STONE ARCH BOOKS:

MEET THE CREATORS!

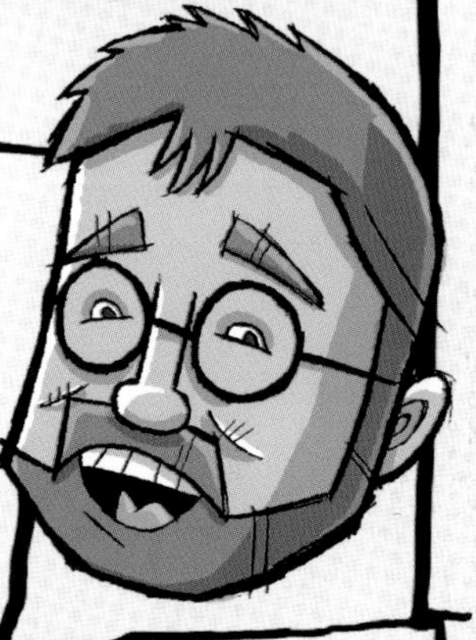

SCOTT NICKEL - AUTHOR

Scott Nickel works by day at Paws, inc., Jim Davis's famous Garfield studio, and he freelances by night. Scott has created hundreds of humorous greeting cards and written several children's books, short fiction for *Boys' Life* magazine, comic strips, and lots of really funny knock-knock jokes. Scott currently lives in Indiana with his wife, two sons, six cats, and several sea monkeys.

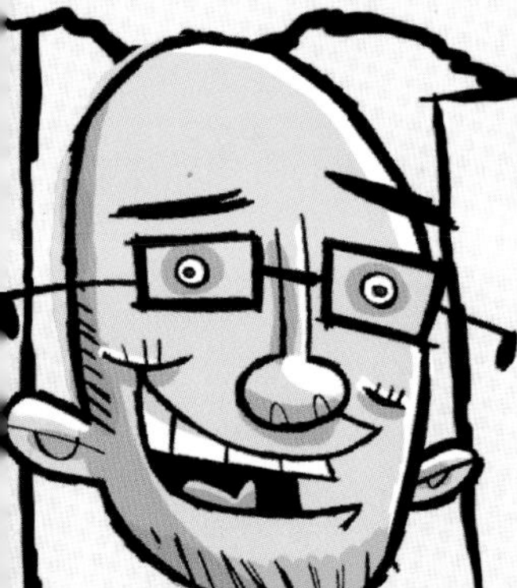

C.S. JENNINGS - ILLUSTRATOR

C.S. Jennings has been a freelance illustrator for over a decade. Jennings has created caricatures, editorial cartoons, greeting cards, t-shirt art, logos, children's books, card games — you name it. He also wrote and illustrated the children's picture book *Animal Band*. In 1994, he won an Addy Award for his work in advertising. He currently lives in Austin, Texas.

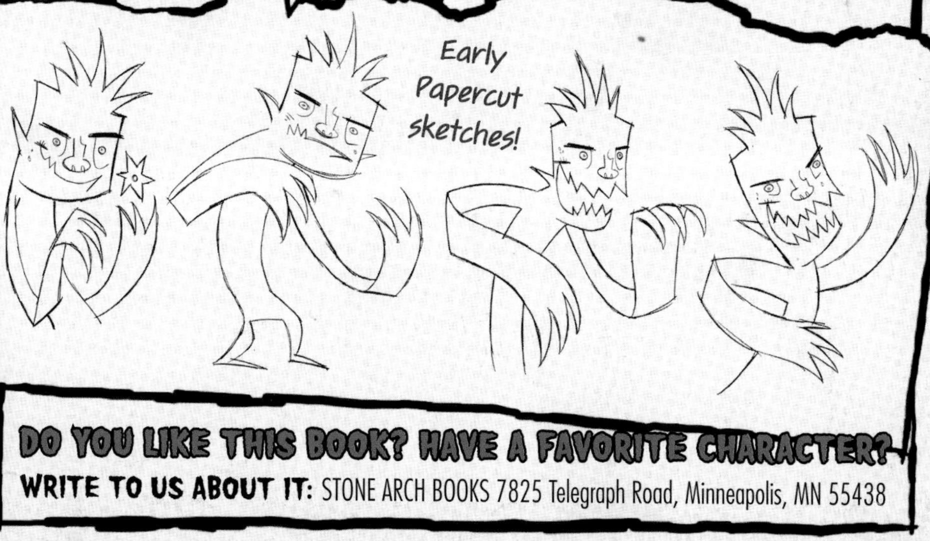
Early Papercut sketches!

DO YOU LIKE THIS BOOK? HAVE A FAVORITE CHARACTER?

WRITE TO US ABOUT IT: STONE ARCH BOOKS 7825 Telegraph Road, Minneapolis, MN 55438

HEY KIDS! IT'S TIME AGAIN FOR...

THE GLOSSARY

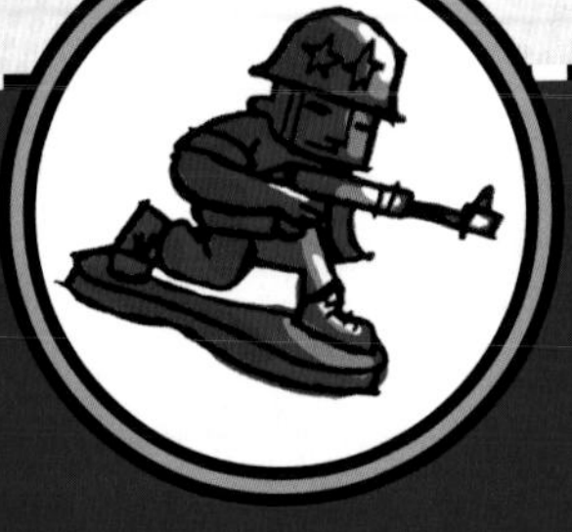

BROUGHT TO YOU BY... THE GENERAL'S NERDY SIDEKICK!

defenseless (di-FENSS-liss)—unable to defend yourself, like when a nerdy kid is attacked by a super-villain

diversion (duh-VUR-zhuhn)—something used to distract others, like shiny objects or candy

obituary (oh-BICH-oo-air-ee)—a notice of the death of a person. Spencer probably would've had to write Chip's obituary if Scissorlegz hadn't saved the day!

origami (or-uh-GAH-mee)—the Japanese art of folding paper into things like a pretty swan or an angry catfish

secret identity (SEE-krit eye-DEN-ti-tee)—if you have a secret identity, you haven't told anyone that you're also a superhero

sidekick (SIDE-kik)—an assistant, or a close friend, who helps you defeat evil, mutant bullies

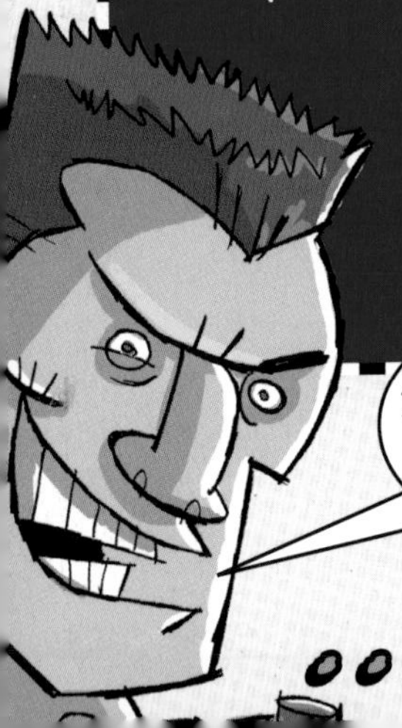
Hmm. Maybe I'll get a SIDEKICK of my own for the next book . . .

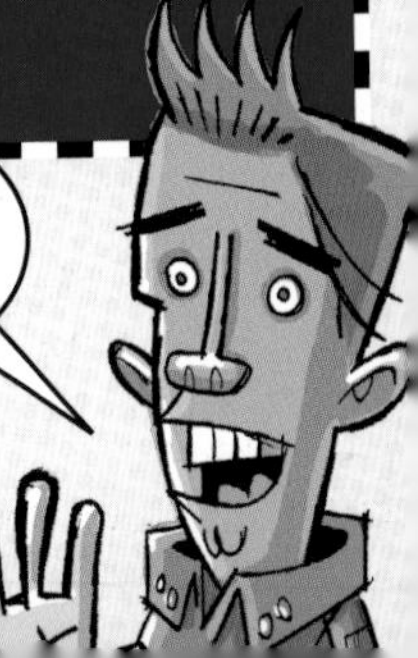
Ooh, pick me, pick me!

...SIGN UP NOW!

K-ROC NEWS 5

QUESTIONS AND PROMPTS

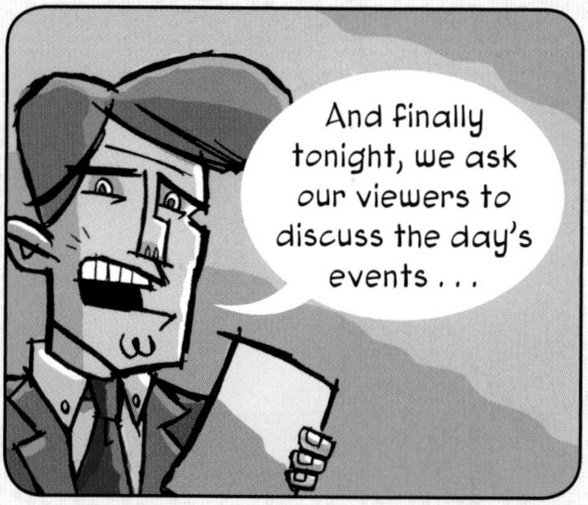
And finally tonight, we ask our viewers to discuss the day's events . . .

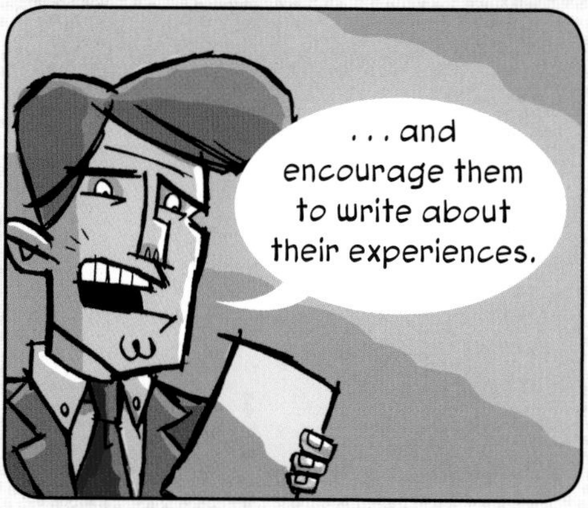
. . . and encourage them to write about their experiences.

1. Who is your favorite character in this book — Rockhead, Scissorlegz, or Papercut? Why?
2. Do you think Papercut will ever return to battle Rockhead again? Why or why not?

1. Troy Perkins, a.k.a. Papercut, is a bully and a super-villain. Which is worse?
2. Create your own superhero. What's his name? What superpowers does he have? Write about him. Then, draw a picture of your superhero!

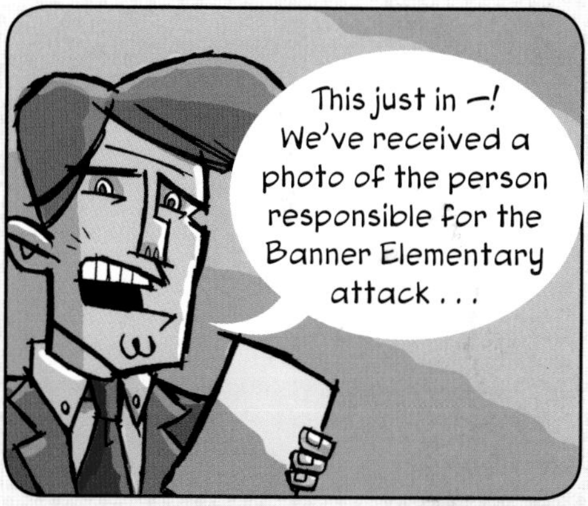
This just in —! We've received a photo of the person responsible for the Banner Elementary attack . . .

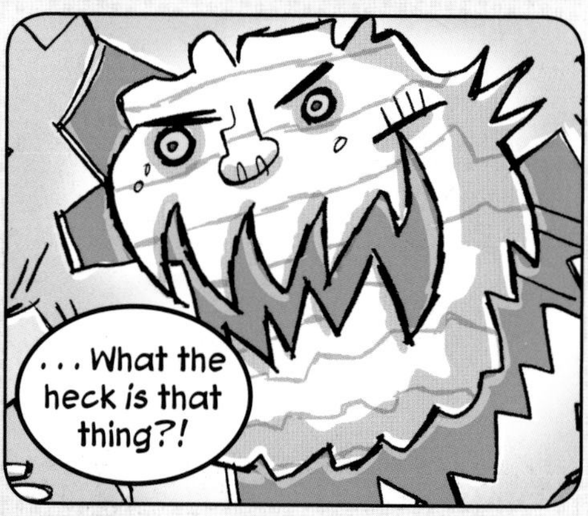
. . . What the heck is that thing?!

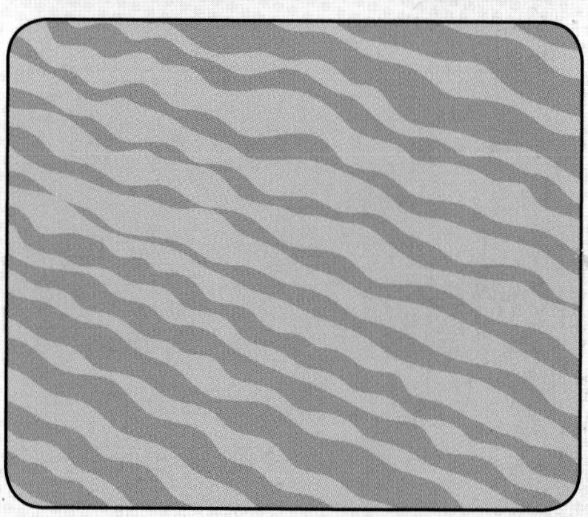

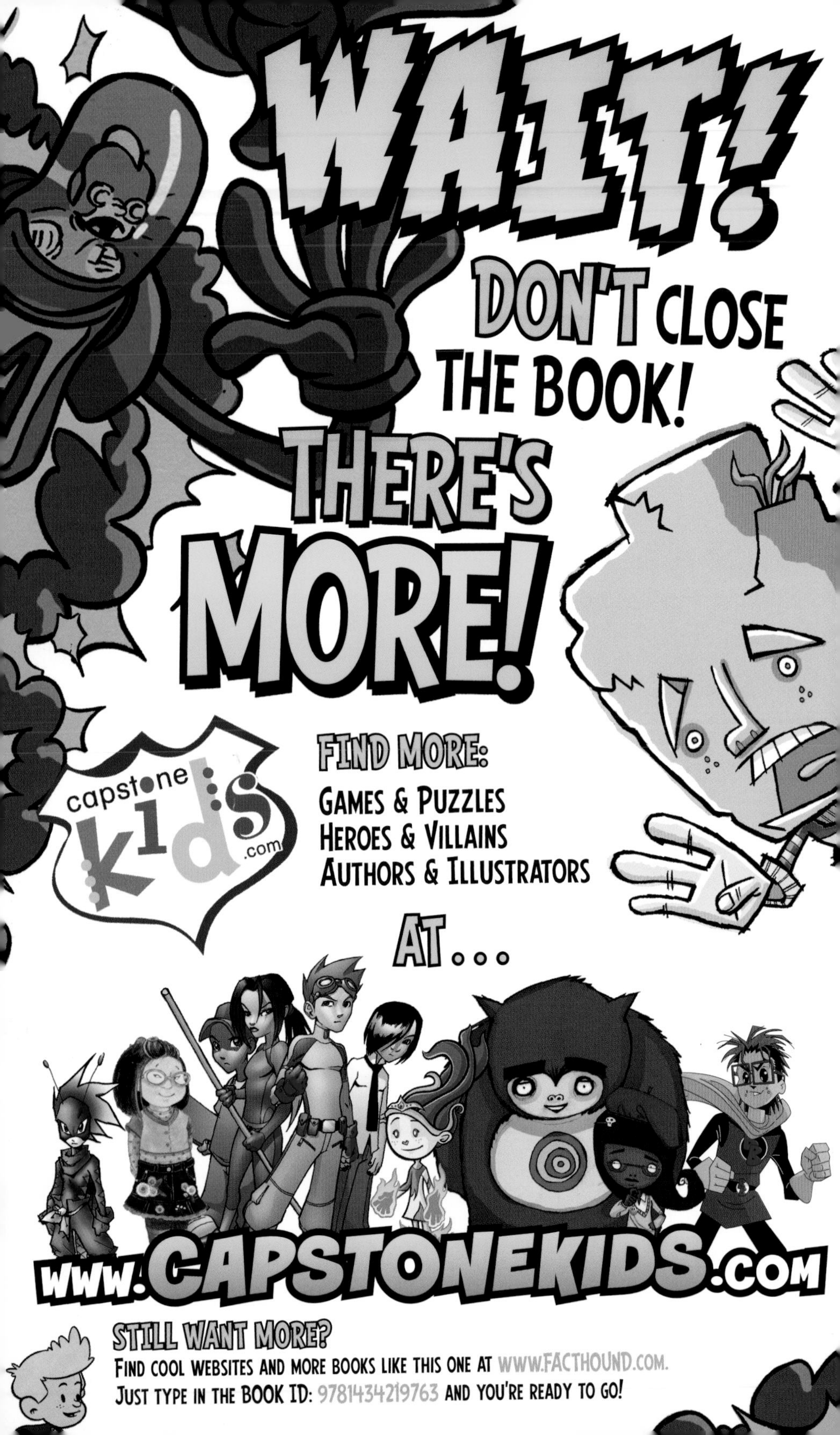
WAIT!
DON'T CLOSE THE BOOK!
THERE'S MORE!
capstone kids .com
FIND MORE:
GAMES & PUZZLES
HEROES & VILLAINS
AUTHORS & ILLUSTRATORS
AT...
WWW.CAPSTONEKIDS.COM
STILL WANT MORE?
FIND COOL WEBSITES AND MORE BOOKS LIKE THIS ONE AT WWW.FACTHOUND.COM.
JUST TYPE IN THE BOOK ID: 9781434219763 AND YOU'RE READY TO GO!